The Adventures of Phoebe Flower

Stories of a Girl with ADHD

By Barbara A. Roberts

Illustrated by Kate Sternberg

ADVANTAGE BOOKS

Washington, DC

Published by Advantage Books. LLC
3268 Arcadia Place, NW
Washington DC 20015

Roberts, Barbara A., 1947–
    Phoebe Flower's adventures : that's what kids are for /
by Barbara A. Roberts ; illustrations by Kate Sternberg.
        p. cm. — (Phoebe Flower's adventures)
    Summary: As she starts second grade, impulsive Phoebe is sure that
she will not be happy.
    ISBN   0-9660366-2-X
    [1. Schools—Fiction.   2. Behavior—Fiction.]
    I. Sternberg, Kate, 1954–   ill.   II. Title.
    III. Series: Roberts, Barbara A., 1947–   Phoebe Flower's adventures.
    PZ7.R5395Ph   1998
    [E]—dc21

10 9 8 7 6 5 4 3 2 1
Printed in the U.S.A.

I would like to dedicate this book to my family
Carly—my edification
Nathan—my inspiritaion
Megan—my visualization
Michael—my foundation
Without their love and support this book would
not be possible.

And to my many friends who have encouraged me.
I would also like to give a special thanks to Suzanne—
my motivation.   B.R.

To Cozy & Beryl / Ken & Tom
and
My Sunrise Valley Family

K.S.

Part 1

That's What
Kids Are For

Don't Make Me, Please!

"Get up, get up, get up!" cries my mother as she kisses my forehead. "Today is the first day of second grade, Phoebe. You're going to love second grade. It was my favorite grade. You are really going to love it. I feel it in my heart. I just know it."

"Oh, ooh, no," I moan. "Don't make me get up. Please, don't make me. I won't like second grade. And worse than that, second grade won't like me. I couldn't even force myself to think about going to second grade this summer. I don't like school. I won't like second grade. I have no friends and I don't want any."

I slide underneath the covers, turn around so my head is at the bottom of my bed and put my feet on the pillows. "Tell my teacher you couldn't find me."

"But Phoebe, remember how we searched all over the mall for that perfect pair of faded blue jeans. Then we finally found them and I bought them for you even though they cost me way too much money? Remember you couldn't wait to wear them, but you knew they were too perfect to wear for just any old day? Those faded blue jeans have been waiting in your closet for the first day of second grade," explains my mother. "Hurry and get up. Put on those new faded blue jeans and make them happy. They have been waiting for this day. Hurry, Phoebe, the bus will be here very soon."

I drag myself out of bed, look in the mirror at a very sad second grade face, and yell, "Okay, I'll make those faded blue jeans happy. I'll go to school and I'll show everybody that I was right. Second grade will not like me."

I pull on my new faded blue jeans, and my brand new dinosaur tee shirt. Then I drag myself down the hall to the breakfast table. I sit staring at my plate. "What are these two yellow eyeballs doing on my plate?" I ask.

"I always make fried eggs on the first day of school. Do you want jelly on your toast?" my mother asks me. "By the way, Phoebe, Amanda already ate her breakfast and . . . her bus comes fifteen minutes after yours. She loved her eggs. She wants me to make them every day."

Amanda is my older sister and, of course, she already ate her breakfast. She always does what she's supposed to do. In a word . . . Amanda is perfect. She's thirteen, sort of pretty, I guess, and everybody thinks she's brilliant, except me. I think she's a royal pain in the neck. She will make a great mother, someday, that's for sure, because she's had a lot of practice. She thinks she's thirty-two years old.

"Don't you remember the last time I tried to eat a fried egg and the egg got caught in the back of my throat and I couldn't swallow and I thought I would choke and die?" I ask. No one answers.

I try again. "How can anyone eat on the first day of school?" Amanda looks at me and smiles like a thirty-two year old mother and says, "A good hearty breakfast is necessary for your brain, Phoebe. And, by the way, I think you should be more dressed up. You should definitely wear a skirt on the first day of school."

I don't know why I ever talk to her.

"How come Walter gets to eat oatmeal for breakfast?" I ask mom. Walter is my baby brother. He has oatmeal all over his face. He's two years old and I know he likes me. When I make a funny face he laughs at me and says, "Up, Fee Fee. Up, Fee Fee." Then I pick him up and make more funny faces.

"Babies eat oatmeal, Phoebe, and don't worry about Walter. Worry about yourself. Are you finished with breakfast?" asks my mother. "R.V. is already on the corner waiting for the school bus. It'll be coming any minute."

My Only Friend

R.V. is Robert Vaughn III. He lives across the street from me. I call
him Robbie. His family and close friends call him R.V., but not me. I used
to call him R.V. until one day my mother told me how Mr. and Mrs.
Spencer, our neighbors who live next door, bought an R. V. and were
going to California. I thought Robbie's parents had sold him to the Spencers because they didn't have any kids. Then finally I asked my mom if
she would ever sell me to the Spencers if they decided they wanted a
girl and she said, "What on earth are you talking about?"

"Well, they bought Robbie, didn't they?" I asked. "He hasn't been in
school for a week and you told me they bought R.V."

I don't think I ever saw my mother laugh so hard. "No, sweetie," my
mom said, "R.V., oops, I mean Robbie, has the chicken pox and that's
why he's been out of school. The Spencers bought a Recreational Ve-
hicle. People call it an R.V. for short. It's a big camper that they can use

to go camping. I would never sell you, Phoebe, not for all the money in the world."

Well, that was then, and this is now, and when my mom finds out how much second grade hates me she will probably sell me for an M & M.

"Phoebe, I am talking to you. Did you eat anything? The bus is coming very soon so please take a bite of toast and hurry up. I don't want to drive you to school on the first day," pleads my mom as she leans over the sink to look out the window for the bus.

"This is your last chance, Mom. I can stay home and help you vacuum and dust. I can polish your silverware. You know how you say you never get a chance to polish your silverware. When you want to use it for Thanksgiving you can't because it looks so yucky. What d'ya say?" I beg and fall to my knees.

"Goodbye, Phoebe," says Amanda, with a disgusting smile on her face.

"Kiss me goodbye, Phoebe," says my mother wrapping her arms around my neck and squeezing me so tight I can't talk. "Remember, I have a good feeling about second grade. It'll be a great year."

I grab my book bag and my lunch and head out the front door. "Yuck to second grade!" I say to Buddy Dog as I pat his head on the way out the door. "I wish I was a dog."

Buddy Dog stretches his hind legs and peeks up at me under his bushy bangs. "I'm sure he was thinking, 'And I'm very glad I am a dog.'"

Mom was right, Robbie was on the corner waiting for the school bus. He had on a brown tie and shiny brown shoes. Amanda must have called his mother and told her that Robbie should get dressed up on the first day of school. Robbie has bright red hair and lots of freckles. He's my only friend. I don't know if it's because he has no other friends or

11

because he really likes me. He likes to pick up worms and he knows how to make the greatest snowmen.

"Hi, Robbie, how come you're at the bus stop so early?" I shout at him as I cross the street. "Don't tell me you want to go to school."

"Well, sort of, Phoebe," Robbie answers. "Summer was getting pretty boring and my mom says that second grade is the best grade of all. I hope we're in the same room."

"Nobody says summer is boring, Robbie. You must be getting the chicken pox again," I tell him, feeling annoyed that his mom said the same thing about second grade as my mom did. Was that just a "mom thing" to say?

A Bad Bus Day

I see the bus coming around the corner. It pulls up and makes a loud sighing noise before it stops. The bus probably hates going to school, too. Robbie jumps on the bus first, runs down the aisle and sits in the farthest seat in the back. I start back there too. I like to sit in the back seat. No one can see me there and sometimes I wave and make faces at the cars behind the bus. When I find Robbie he smiles a "Sorry, Phoebe, there's no more room here," smile. "Just great," I think out loud, as I start to walk backwards up the aisle looking to the left and right, desperately trying to find somewhere to sit.

"Please take a seat!" the bus driver yells.

I'm almost back up to the front of the bus when I finally see an empty seat next to the window. "Could you please move over?" I say as nicely as I can to the curly haired girl sitting next to the empty seat.

"No!" she answers without looking at me.

"What's your name?" yells the bus driver.

"Phoebe," I whisper back. I feel my face getting hot.

"Well, Phoebe, sit down now!"

I climb over the curly haired girl and plop down just as the bus takes off.

"Phoebe, that's a funny name. How do you even spell it?" she says. "I have a beautiful name. My name is Elizabeth. And . . . didn't you know you should wear a skirt on the first day of school? I just moved here, and we would never wear dirty old jeans on the first day of school."

My grandmother always says, "If you can't think of anything nice to say, don't say anything at all."

So the rest of the ride I don't say one word but I do think about my name. It is hard to spell and that's another reason I don't like school. I'd like to spell it FeeBee because that's alot easier to remember. I told my first grade teacher, Mrs. Ward, and she said "Now that you're in school, Phoebe, you have to spell your name the correct way. You don't want to start a bad habit do you?"

After what seems like a zillion days the bus door opens. I can finally get away from that awful Elizabeth. When I get off the bus, Robbie is nowhere to be found. I see a list in the hall that says, Phoebe Flower—room number 24, teacher—Ms. Biz. My mother said she hoped I would get Ms. Biz because Mrs. Spencer's cousin's neighbor had her for second grade and she loved her. She said I would be very lucky to have Ms. Biz because she loves girls. I don't know if that's very lucky.

I have to go past my old first grade room to get to room 24. Maybe I'll stop in and see Mrs. Ward, my first grade teacher, since I'm in no big hurry to meet Ms. Biz. I stick my head in and hear a voice say, "Hi, Phoebe! How was your summer?"

I answer, "Fine, thanks, Mrs. Ward."

"Want to come in and see the monarch chrysalis we have? Remember we had two last year and they changed into the most beautiful butterflies? Remember we let one go and had a freedom, farewell party? Remember we had butterfly crackers with orange marmalade and licorice to remind us of the color of the monarch butterfly?" Mrs. Ward asked.

"Sure," I answer, remembering that I dropped the spoon with

15

the marmalade on my chair and then I sat on it. All day I stuck to every chair that I sat in.

Then Mrs. Ward asked, "Remember that one little girl in the class that couldn't stand to see those butterflies cooped up in the glass bottle and let one go in the classroom and it landed on top of the bookshelf and I had to get the custodian to get it down?" she asks.

"Sure," I said, realizing that Mrs. Ward didn't remember that I was that little girl. "Well, I've got to go find my second grade classroom now. Good luck with those butterflies, Mrs. Ward." I quickly skip out the door just as five new first graders are coming in. I squeeze out between them and continue down the hall looking for room 24.

So ... This Is
Second Grade

"Welcome!" cries a tall, skinny lady with short black hair standing in the doorway of room 24. "You must be Phoebe Flower. I'm Ms. Biz and we've been waiting for you. All the other boys and girls are here. Please find a seat and then we'll take attendance. I just love your jeans, Phoebe."

This might not be too bad. I look around to see who's in my class. Robbie is in the back of the room. He looks at me and waves a tiny wave and points to a seat next to him. Maybe my mom was right. Maybe second grade will be okay.

"Everyone is here today. Isn't that wonderful?" says Ms. Biz, "I love it when everyone is here. Owen, please pick someone to take the attendance slip to the health office with you."

"Elizabeth," says Owen.

Oh, rats, I didn't even see her. What a way to completely ruin a not-so-great day. She must have been sitting in the seat in front of Ms. Biz's desk.

"We will start today by having everyone tell us one thing they did over the summer. Who would like to begin?" Ms. Biz asks.

Four hands shot up in the air.

"I got a new puppy," says Evan, "and he's all mine. I'm in charge of training him."

"How responsible, Evan! Elaina?" asks Ms. Biz.

"I went to the creek with my brother and caught fourteen fish," Elaina says smiling at Ms. Biz.

"Nice fishing, Elaina! Oh, and I just love the way Owen and Elizabeth walk quietly back from the office and sit down in their seats without a sound." Ms. Biz looks up and smiles at Elizabeth and Owen.

"Jeremy?" Ms. Biz continues to ask about vacations.

"I made a volcano out of soap suds and vinegar and I brought it in to show the class," said Jeremy, "but I'll need some help with it."

"Okay, Jeremy, pick a friend to help you," says Ms. Biz.

"Elizabeth, will you?" asks Jeremy.

"Why do boys always pick the same girl?" I whisper to Robbie. "Elizabeth got picked to go to the health office. Elizabeth, Elizabeth, Elizabeth, yuck!"

"Do you want to share something with the class, Phoebe?" Ms. Biz asks me.

"No thank you!" I answer. "I'm still thinking."

Second grade was just what I thought. I'm happy that Robbie's in my class, but mad as heck that Elizabeth is too. Not only do all the boys like Elizabeth, but so does Ms. Biz. I can tell already that it will be "Elizabeth this" and "Elizabeth that" all year.

When it was my turn to tell about my summer vacation, I said, "I spent a week with my dad."

"Big deal," Elizabeth turned around in her seat and whispered, "I spend every day with my dad."

I couldn't wait to go home. I missed fifteen minutes of play time because I didn't finish my math. I didn't finish it for two reasons. One reason was I simply hate math. I just don't get it. Just because there were only six problems to do didn't matter. It seemed like six hundred. The second reason was I happened to pick a wobbly desk to sit in and when I bent over to put a book under the wobble part of my desk I noticed my sneaker was untied so of course I had to tie it because I could trip and kill myself. Then as I was tying it I wondered how many times I could tie my sneaker until I ran out of shoe lace. I could tie it six times and still have a

little shoe lace left. Ms. Biz didn't care. She said, "Phoebe, you cannot go outside for playtime if your math isn't finished. I don't care how many times you tied your sneaker."

My first day in second grade is almost over. I start to count the minutes until the bus will come and take me home. Finally, twelve minutes and thirteen seconds are left until the bell rings.

"May I have your attention?" Ms. Biz announces. "Over the summer, boys and girls, every teacher received two hundred dollars to spend on supplies for their classroom. I spent my money on entertainment. On the shelf you will find what you may think are toys, but I prefer to think of these items as entertainment. You will have ten minutes to look at the new items I purchased and tomorrow you will have more time to entertain yourself with them. Walk over to the shelves. Do not run, and please share."

That's Entertainment

Who cares? In about ten minutes and four seconds I'll be on the bus to home sweet home. I skip over to the shelf to have a look, anyway, just in case there's something good, but I doubt it. Robbie got to the shelf first.

"Hey, Robbie, what'd ya find to entertain with?" I ask him.

"This is so cool, Phoebe, it's a magnifying glass. Watch this!" he answers.

Robbie runs over to the fish bowl and covers his eye with the magnifying glass. "Look, there's no fish in here anymore. There are only whales." He runs to the gerbil cage. "Hey, everybody, come and look at the dinosaur." Robbie walks toward me and stares right at me for a long time. "Phoebe, you look so much older. You look like you're nine now, instead of eight."

"Let me see, let me see!" everyone yells at Robbie.

"Boys and girls!" calls Ms. Biz. "There is always tomorrow. It's time to get your book bags and line up to go home now."

Out of the corner of my eye, I see something red. I look again and can't believe it. Ms. Biz ordered an Etch-a-Sketch! I love Etch-a-Sketch. I had one when I was five and I could make the neatest house. I'll try it for just a minute. I grab it off the shelf and sit on the beanbag chair behind the bookshelf. I'll only be a minute. I just want to see if I can remember how to make a house.

Well, the next thing I remember is, "Phoebe Flower, you missed your bus! What are you doing?" Ms. Biz was standing over me with a very red face. I could tell she was mad.

"Well, I saw this entertainment, Ms. Biz, and I thought I would just try to see if I could remember how to make a house like I did when I was five. I had an Etch-a-Sketch when I was five. I just had to put the roof on the house and then it would be finished. It was just going to be a minute." I try to explain.

22

"Phoebe, you missed your bus and now you have to go to the principal's office and she will have to call your mother to come and get you. The principal will not be happy. Your mother will not be happy and I am not happy." Ms. Biz was talking pretty loudly.

"Sorry," I say, "but I only had to put the roof on." "Grab your book bag, Phoebe. Walk, do not skip, to the office and tell Dr. Nicely what happened," says Ms. Biz.

"Dr. Nicely, who's that?" I ask Ms. Biz.

"Dr. Nicely is our new principal, Phoebe, and like I said, Dr. Nicely will not be happy to have to call your mother on the first day of school."

I walk baby steps to the office. What's a doctor doing in school? I wonder. Maybe he'll take out my tonsils 'cause I missed the bus. Maybe he's a dentist. Maybe he pulls a tooth each time a kid misses the bus. Maybe I'll just run out the front door and never come back. I hear high heel footsteps coming down the hall. It has to be Ms. Biz coming to see if I went in the office yet. I push open the office door.

"Hi, Phoebe!" says Mrs. Walkerspeaking, the school secretary. I know her pretty well from last year. Robbie insists her name is just Mrs. Walker, but I know her better than he does because I spent a lot of time in the office when I was in kindergarten and when I was in first grade. Every morning when she would get on the loud speaker she would say, "Good morning, boys and girls, this is Mrs. Walkerspeaking!" and every time she answered the telephone she would always say, "Hello, Mrs. Walkerspeaking."

"Hi," I mumble back.

"How's second grade going?" she asks.

"Do you know what an Etch-a-Sketch is, Mrs. Walkerspeaking? Well, I was just going to make a house like I did when I was five years old. I

23

couldn't figure out how to put the roof on because triangles aren't easy to make. I didn't hear Ms. Biz. call my bus number. I was only going to be a minute and now Ms. Biz is mad at me and the Doctor is going to be mad at me and my mother is going to be mad and I'm going to have my teeth pulled out. I just want to go home."

"My name is Mrs. Walker, and yes, sure, I remember Etch-a-Sketch, Phoebe. I always had trouble with triangles too. Wait here," smiles Mrs. Walkerspeaking. "I'll go get Dr. Nicely."

I decided to go look in my book bag for an old cough drop. Maybe if I smell sick he'll feel sorry for me and won't pull my teeth. If he comes out of that office with plastic gloves and a white coat on, I am running out that door as fast as I can until I get to Alaska.

24

Dr. Who?

"Hello, Phoebe, I'm Dr. Nicely." says a voice that sounds like my Aunt Mary. I bite my lip hard so I won't cry and when I look up I see eyes that are the color of my favorite crayon, blue-green-purple. Dr. Nicely has on high heels and a blue-green-purple dress and blue-green-purple earrings. She looks like the lady that does the six o'clock news.

"Are you a doctor? Are you going to pull out my teeth?" I ask.

"No, Phoebe, I'm not going to pull your teeth. Come into my office and we'll talk." Dr. Nicely smiles.

"Well, I just want you to know I already told my mom that second grade wouldn't like me. She won't be surprised. It's not my fault. It really isn't. I didn't even want to be entertained. I just wanted to be home," I tell the doctor.

We walk together into Dr. Nicely's office.

"Are those all yours?" I ask pointing to the puppets lined up on the shelf over her desk.

"Yes, Phoebe, I collect puppets and marionettes," she answers. "Someday I'll come into your classroom and do a little show for your class and you can meet some of my friends on the shelf. Now, tell me why you missed your bus."

"Well . . . do you know what an Etch-a-Sketch is? Well . . . I just wanted to see if I could make a house like I did when I was five. I remember that I made a good house when I was five and I was just going to be a minute, but then I couldn't figure out how to make the roof. Even Mrs. Walkerspeaking knows that roofs are hard to make. She said she always had trouble with roofs. Anyway, I kept getting all messed up and I was

26

only going to be a minute and I didn't hear Ms. Biz call my bus and now she is mad and my mother will be mad and you're going to pull out my teeth and I'm going to run away to Alaska," I say in one breath.

"I had an Etch-a-Sketch, too, Phoebe, and I was awful at making houses. My sister, though, she could make everything. She could make people with round heads. She could even write her name in cursive in a straight line." Dr. Nicely whispers to me, "If I tell you a secret, will you promise not to tell anyone?"

I look straight into those blue-green-violet eyes and answer, "I promise on a cross-my-heart. I will never, not even if someone pulls out all my teeth, Dr. Nicely. It will be our secret until death," I bravely tell her.

"Well, one day my sister made an Etch-a-Sketch picture of the whole family. She made arms and legs and fingers and toes. It was a real beauty. Then when I saw my sister go into the bathroom, I snuck into her room and shook the picture until it was gone. She never knew I did it." Dr. Nicely sighs.

"Wow!" I breathe. "Was she sad?"

"Oh, sure, and I felt terrible after I shook it but I was so jealous that I couldn't do Etch-a- Sketch like she could," Dr. Nicely says with a very sad face. "Remember Phoebe, this is our secret.'

"For sure, Dr. Nicely, for sure," I promise.

"And, I understand why you missed your bus, Phoebe," says Dr. Nicely, "but I will have to call your mother to come and pick you up and she will be not be happy. Does your mother work, Phoebe?"

"Yes, she brushes people's teeth at the dentist office, but she makes me brush my own," I explain.

"Well, you'll have to wait out in the office with Mrs. Walker until your mother comes, Phoebe, and give her this note. Keep practicing that

Etch-a-Sketch, too, but please listen when your teacher calls the buses." Dr. Nicely sounds serious, but she still smiles at me.

I had to wait a half hour for my mom to come and pick me up. Ms. Biz was right. My mother was not happy. In fact, she didn't say one word until we got home. She opened the note that Dr. Nicely gave me and I could tell my mother didn't really care that much about my Etch-a-Sketch problem. "Don't let this happen again, Phoebe. I'll lose my job if I have to leave work early again."

For the next two days I tried so hard to be good at school. Ms. Biz actually asked me to take a message to the library and I made sure I walked straight there and straight back.

Rainbow Feet and
Toilet Fish

Then on the third day . . .

"Please, Phoebe, not another note from school!" says my mother. "I am very upset!"

"But Mom, I try to be good," I answer.

"I know you try, Phoebe, but today's note says, "Dear Mrs. Flower, Phoebe got into trouble today. She walked on the paintings that were drying in the hall and then continued to walk down the hall leaving blue and purple footprints zigzagging all the way to the library. Please speak to her about her behavior," Mother reads.

"But, Mom, let me explain what really happened," I moan.

"What happened then, Phoebe?" asks my mom, as she sinks into her chair.

"Well, Elaina was line leader of the week. She forgot to take the note the teacher told her to take to give to the librarian, so I hurried to the front of the line to remind her. I said, very politely of course, "Excuse me,

Elaina, you forgot the note you were supposed to take," and Elaina thought I was budging her. She ignored me, so I had to move out into the hall to show her that I was trying to help her. Of course I didn't know that wet painted pictures were in the hall so I stepped on them. I didn't know that there was paint on my shoes when I walked down the hall to the library either." I stop to take a breath.

"Well, that makes sense, Phoebe," says my mother, "but please think about what you are doing. "

"Listen, Phoebe," said Amanda, as she walked into the living room from the kitchen, "I didn't mean to overhear your problem, but I did. Here's just a little lesson from your big sister. You should have minded your own business. Let Ms. Biz tell Elaina what to do. That's what teachers are for, you know."

I sigh. Sometimes I really don't like my sister and I really hate school. I've only made one other friend than Robbie and that's Jack, the class gerbil. I'm the only one who can feed Jack from my hand. The other kids are afraid of Jack and Jack seems to know I'm not. At bedtime after my mom puts Walter to bed, she comes into my room and hugs me. "I love you, Phoebe," she says. "Please try not to get in trouble at school tomor-row."

"Don't worry," I promise, "from now on, no more notes."

Two days later . . .

"I thought you said no more notes, Phoebe," my mother says. "What does this one say?" "Dear Mrs. Flower, Phoebe got into trouble today. She put our class goldfish in the toilet bowl. I am very surprised, as she is so kind to our gerbil, Jack. In fact, Phoebe is the only one who can feed Jack from her hand. Phoebe needs to think about her behavior. Please speak to her!"

30

My eyes fill with tears as I say, "But, Mom, let me explain what really happened."

"What really happened, Phoebe?" asks my mom, as she plops deep into her chair.

"Well, I didn't know that the teacher was cleaning the fish tank and, of course, I asked why this fish was in a little paper cup and, of course, no one answered me because no one likes me except Jack, so I took that fish in that little paper cup, and I said to myself I am going to give that fish some room to swim, so I put that fish in the toilet bowl so he could have some room to really swim around." I pause.

"I am trying to understand, Phoebe, but you need to go to your room and think about what you did," says my mother. "And please, NO MORE NOTES FROM SCHOOL!"

I run to my room and throw myself on my bed. "School stinks" I say over and over again. I can't wait until I'm a grown-up and never have to go to school again.

I hear a knock as my bedroom door pushes open. "Phoebe, it's me," says Amanda. "I really didn't mean to eavesdrop, but I heard Mom yell at you. This is just a little big-sisterly advice. Let Ms. Biz clean the fish bowl by herself. That's what teachers are for, you know."

"Get out of my room, Amanda," I tell her as my eyes fill up with tears.

We eat dinner without saying much to each other. Walter tries to make us laugh by making funny noises, but Amanda tells him not to make noises with his mouth full. At bedtime, after my mother puts Walter to bed, she comes into my room and rocks me in her arms and sings her favorite songs. "Don't worry, Mom," I say, yawning. "This time, I promise, no more notes."

That's What Kids Are For

The very next day . . .

"Phoebe, you said, no more notes. YOU PROMISED, NO MORE NOTES," loudly moans my mother. "This note says. 'Dear Mrs. Flower, PHOEBE GOT INTO BIG TROUBLE TODAY! SHE DIDN'T SIT AT HER DESK. SHE SAT UNDER IT WITH HER FEET ON THE SEAT. SHE DIDN'T WRITE HER NAME ON HER PAPER. SHE DREW HER PICTURE INSTEAD. Phoebe needs to think about her behavior. Please speak to her.'" My mother crumples up the note and throws it in the basket.

"That's it!! No more T.V.! No more ANYTHING!" cries my mother.

"But Mom, let me tell you what really happened," I cry. "What really happened then, Phoebe?" says my mother, looking totally exhausted as she fell into the chair.

"Well, Robbie wanted to borrow my pencil and the point was pretty dull, so I raised my hand to ask Ms. Biz if I could sharpen it. Of course, she didn't see me, so I looked in my desk for a sharp pencil and I couldn't find one. I had to sit on the floor to get a better look into my desk and then I got tired. I wanted to put my feet up and there was nowhere to put my feet except on my chair. No one would have known, except Elizabeth had to tell the teacher that I was sitting on the floor with my feet on the chair. Then, because I gave Robbie my only pencil, I couldn't write my name too well so I thought that I should draw my picture because I draw my picture much better than I write my name."

"I am trying to understand, Phoebe. I am trying really hard . . . but this time I mean it. . . not one more note," begs my mother. "Please think before you act."

"No more notes," I repeat. "This time I really truly promise."

I go outside and sit on the swing. Buddy dog bounces over and sniffs me. "I really don't mean to do these things, Buddy dog. I just forget. Then everybody always gets mad at me. Can I come and live in your doghouse with you?"

"Woof," barks Buddy dog.

"Phoebe," calls Amanda.

Oh great, a little sisterly advice, just what I want to hear, I think to myself. "I'm not here," I answer.

"Phoebe," Amanda walks over to the swing set and starts to speak, "just a little big-sisterly advice, next time tell Robbie to ask the teacher for a pencil. That's what teachers are for, you know."

"Thank you, Amanda, next time I will," I say staring right at her and remembering what my grandmother said about not saying anything if you can't think of anything nice to say.

At bedtime that night, my mother and I snuggle together as we read a book. My mother hugs me tightly and says, "I know you have a hard time sitting still, Phoebe. I know you don't always think before you do something. I really do understand. I didn't want to tell you this, but I had a hard time in school too. I used to say a little rhyme to myself when I had trouble concentrating. It went like this:

Think, think
It's good for the brain.
And your teachers and friends
Won't think you're a pain.

Please try harder and remember I love you very much."
"Thanks, Mom, I'll try that," I say. "I love you too!"

One week later . . . "Oh no! I knew it was too good to be true. It's been a whole week without a note, Phoebe," says my mother. Slowly, very slowly, my mom opens the note. "Dear Mrs. Flower," she reads out loud. "Phoebe has had a great day."

"Today, Phoebe was a heroine. Robbie let Jack out of his cage. Jack jumped out of our window and ran across the playground toward the flagpole in the front of the school. Just as the custodian began to raise the flag for the day, Jack leaped onto the flag and his claws became stuck. The custodian didn't see him and Jack rode up to the top of the pole. Without thinking about it, Phoebe ran to the flagpole, shimmied up to the top, picked up Jack, put him on her shoulder, and slid back down. The whole class watched with amazement. When Phoebe came down we all clapped for her wonderful rescue. You should be very proud of Phoebe."

"Phoebe, I am so proud of you," laughs my mother as she hugs me. "You are a true heroine."

"But Mom, let me tell you what really happened," I say.

"What really happened, Phoebe?" asks my mother.

"My teacher said I didn't think about it. I did think about it. I just wanted to save Jack." I smile and give my mother a big hug.

Then, as fast as I can, I leap up the stairs, two steps at a time, to Amanda's bedroom. I knock and open her bedroom door. "Amanda," I say, as I fold my arms across my chest, "just a little sisterly advice for my big sister. If you want to be a heroine, don't wait for the teacher to do it. That's what kids are for."

Part 2

That's What
Hugs Are For

Dancing High

Being a heroine was great . . . for two days, anyway. The news of how I, Phoebe Flower, shimmied up the flag pole and rescued Jack, our class gerbil, spread throughout the school. Dr. Nicely, the school principal, stopped by my classroom and gave me a gold sticker that said, **"YOU ARE SPECIAL"** and shook my hand.

Ms. Biz, my teacher, said to me, "Phoebe, as a reward, you have my permission to take Jack home for the weekend."

When I got home, I was excited to set up Jack's cage. Buddy Dog sniffed around Jack and made strange growling noises. I think Buddy Dog was jealous of Jack.

Robbie, my best friend, cheered, "High five me, Phoebe. You're terrific!"

Walter, my two year old brother said, "Yea, Fee Fee," and clapped his hands whenever I came near him.

I even heard my sister, Amanda, who thinks she was born for one reason only . . . to be my boss, tell her friend on the phone, "You know, it was my sister who was the second grade heroine."

Mom couldn't stop smiling. She told me I had to call my dad who lives in New York City and tell him. Mom and Dad were divorced two years ago, but they still talk to each other.

I tried to make Mom think she was forcing me to call my dad. I really wanted to call him, but I said, "Oh no, I can't bother Daddy with this little teeny weeny bit of news."

"Little teeny weeny bit of news!" gasped my mother. "Are you kidding? You are a heroine, Phoebe, and this is no little tiny bit of news." Amanda rolled her eyes to the ceiling.

When I finally got Dad on the phone, he thought I was wonderful too. "What a girl, I have! I am so proud of you. You are a brave little girl, Phoebe Flower," he shouted into the phone. But my Grandma Wig was the happiest person of all when I told her my good news. Grandma Wig is my mother's mother and she lives three blocks from us. She got her name, Grandma Wig, from Amanda. Grandma's real name is Gert, but one day Grandma was coming to visit and Mom called Amanda and me together and said, "Girls, Grandma Gert is coming over to visit and she is wearing a wig. Don't say a word about it. Don't even look at her head. She thinks it looks just like real hair and we don't want her to think that we know it isn't. OK?"

"OK, Mom, not a word," we both promised.

When Grandma Gert walked in the door, Amanda and I both stared right at her head and then Amanda said, "Hi, Grandma Wig, you look very nice today."

My mom and my grandma burst out laughing. Amanda turned red

in the face and my Grandma Gert has been Grandma Wig ever since. I think it's the only time that Amanda has ever made a mistake in her whole life.

I really think Grandma Wig likes me better than she likes Walter and Amanda. She almost never gets mad at me and when she comes over to our house she says, "Where is that sweetie, Phoebe?" Grandma Wig made me sit down and tell her the whole story about rescuing Jack. "Please, tell me one more time," she asked after I had already told her twice. I know for sure that I saw a little tear in her eye when she hugged me. "I am so proud of my little sweetie, Phoebe." Then, she said, "You know what I believe, Phoebe? That you'll never dance if you don't take a chance."

Well, after the rescue, I danced all right. For two days I danced. I danced to the bus stop. I danced off the bus. I danced down the halls in school, and I danced to my desk. I danced to lunch, and I danced to gym. Then, after those two very short days of being the heroine of the school, I danced to music class.

Great Advice

My problem with music class began this summer when I had a heart-to-heart talk with Dad. A heart-to-heart talk is a talk that grown-ups want to have with you and they pretend that you want to have it too. I knew that my mom had told my dad that I didn't want to go to second grade. She had tried to get me to talk about my feelings, but I wouldn't say one word about school.

I remember the phone call. It was the hottest day of the summer. Robbie and I were sitting on my front step watching our popsicles drip into puddles and deciding whether to go swimming or just squirt each other with the hose.

"Phoebe!" Mom called me, "Come in the house. Your dad's on the phone. He wants to talk to you. Make sure you listen carefully to what he says."

My mother has never asked me to listen to anything my father said before. My brain was saying, "Phoebe , alert, alert, something's up!"

I sucked in the last mouthful of popsicle and walked into the kitchen with my head aching from the pain of the cold. "Hello, Dad," I said into the phone, trying to figure out what he was going to say that I had to listen to carefully.

From the first word of our conversation, I knew it was going to be a heart-to-heart. "Crazy as this may sound, Phoebe," started my dad, "I didn't always like school either. However, that changed for me when I realized one thing. Phoebe, are you listening to me?"

"Yes, I am, Dad," I answered, puffing short breaths into the phone. I had been twisting and turning as I talked on the phone, and had wrapped the phone cord around my whole body about eleven times.

"Are you okay, Phoebe? You sound out of breath," Dad asked with concern in his voice.

"Fine, Dad," I answered trying to sound fine. I knew I had better listen to my dad or he would tell me the same story over and over again and Mom would come and see if everything was all right and get mad at me for being tangled up.

"I totally agree with you, Father," I answered.

My dad started to tell me about his days at school when he was my age and how hard it was for him to pay attention to the teacher. "You have to be determined, Phoebe," my dad continued. "It's a big word that means that you have to keep on trying and believing that you can do anything you want to do. I mean that, Phoebe. I know you better than anyone else, except your mother, of course, and I know you can do anything if you try hard enough. You have to believe that, too."

I was so happy to be untangled from the phone cord that I didn't realize my dad had stopped talking. After a minute of silence, I said, "Dad, are you still there?"

"Well, Phoebe?" Dad asked.

"I totally agree, Father," I answered again.

"Well . . . then, what is it that you agree to do? What are you going to be determined to do in second grade?" he asked me.

Yikes! My dad wanted an answer right then. I could feel myself start to twist the phone cord around my body again. "Let me have a minute to think about it, Dad. I want to be really sure," I answered .

So I thought and I thought for what seemed like two days. Then, I remembered how I wanted to be Gloria Von Kloppenstein in first grade when she sang all by herself in the first grade chorus at the end of the year. Yes! Yes! That's it!

"Dad, I know what I want to do. I want to sing a solo all by myself in the second grade chorus at the end of the year. I want to see the whole audience stand and clap and cheer. Dad, I want to sing. That's just what I will be determined to do," I answered.

"You want to sing a solo, Phoebe?" my dad asked. "Can you sing?"

"Yep, that's it, Dad. Of course, I can sing. I think I can sing. No, of course, I can sing. Everybody can sing. Thanks for the advice. I feel like a brand new kid. I love you, Dad."

"Goodbye, Phoebe, I love you, too," Dad said quietly.

I untwisted the cord from my body like a ballerina and danced out to the front porch to tell Robbie I was ready to go swimming.

Do-Re-Me

So, here I am dancing into music class and suddenly I remember what my dad and I talked about on the phone that hot summer day. I am Phoebe Flower, the school heroine. I am determined! I can do anything I want. I can sing. I can sing a solo all by myself in the second grade concert at the end of the year.

"Good afternoon, boys and girls!" says Miss Fasola.

"Good afternoon, Miss FASOLA!" we all answer.

"Remember, boys and girls, it's Miss Prissy FASOLA," she reminds us. "Now let's do that again."

"Good afternoon, Miss Prissy FASOLA," we all chant.

"Much, much better, class," she smiles.

Miss Prissy Fasola has black curly hair and black dirt under her eyes. When she smiles, she doesn't show her teeth. She doesn't smile a lot. She is in love with her name. She must be the only teacher in the whole wide world that tells kids her first name. I remember last year in first grade when Robbie told Mrs. Ward, our first grade teacher, that he heard his mother talking and he knew that her first name was Shirley. Mrs. Ward said, "My name is Mrs. Ward, and that's that, Robert!"

"Before we begin our class we will sing the scale," Miss Prissy Fasola says. "Remember, we sing softly until we get to my name and then we sing out loud in our best voices. Ready? Wait for the note that tells us to begin. One, two, three, go!"

We all start to sing softly, "do-re-me." Then the class gets louder on "FA-SO-LA" and then we quietly finish with "ti-do."

"Very nice, boys and girls, but someone was singing a little too loudly. Please, remember, a good voice does not have to be a loud voice," Miss Prissy Fasola grins.

Now that I know I can sing, I do agree with Miss Fasola. A good voice doesn't have to be a loud one. But if I am going to sing a solo all by myself in the second grade concert at the end of the year, I better let Miss Prissy Fasola know that I have a good voice. If I sing softly, she'll never hear me.

"Now, boys and girls," Miss Prissy Fasola claps her hands, "we will practice the song 'America the Beautiful.' It's one of my favorites. Ready, set, listen for the note to begin."

We all start to sing, "Oh beautiful for spacious skies." Miss Fasola smiles and waves her hands and nods her head.

I start to wonder how Miss Prissy Fasola is going to notice my good singing voice when everyone is singing together. I close my eyes and I start to sing as beautifully as I can, "AMERICA, AMERICA, GOD SHED HIS GRACE ON THEE."

"Everybody STOP!" Miss Prissy Fasola yells and claps her hands.

51

"Somebody is singing off key and way, way, too loud. Who is it?"

We all look around at each other. Nobody says anything. I begin to wonder who it is. I glance at Robbie who is sitting next to me. He starts blinking at me like he has dirt caught in both his eyes. Then he puts his pointer finger up to his lips like he wants me to be quiet. I think he's jealous of my voice.

"OK, let's start once again," Miss Fasola says. "One, two, three and remember, boys and girls, a good voice does not have to be a loud voice."

"Yes, that's true," I think to myself, "but, if she doesn't hear me, how will Miss Prissy Fasola know I have great voice, a great voice that should sing a solo in the second grade concert at the end of the year?"

"Oh beautiful, for spacious skies, for . . ." we all start to sing. Miss Prissy Fasola waves her left hand and smiles without showing her teeth. She starts to walk around the room.

"America, America," the class sings together.

"GOD SHED HIS GRACE ON THEE!" I let it blast out of my mouth.

"That's it, that's it! Stop everyone! I hear the voice now. It's over in that group in the corner of the room." Miss Fasola claps her hands and marches closer to the row where I am sitting.

I start to wonder who it is that's singing off the key. I do know that when Miss Prissy Fasola finds out who it is she'll be mad. She got mad at me once last year when I was in first grade and once was enough. I can see Robbie out of the corner of my eye. He has his hands around his neck like he is choking himself. He is acting so weird today. Maybe he wants me to laugh so I'll get in trouble. Sorry, not today, Robbie. Today, I'm going to be discovered.

"This will be the last time I say this, boys and girls. A good voice does not have to be a loud voice. Everyone will, once again, start from the beginning. I think we are all getting tired of starting from the beginning, aren't we? But, we will do this until we get it right, won't we, boys and girls?"

"Yes, Miss Prissy Fasola!" we all say at the same time.

"One, two, three, go!"

"Oh beautiful, for spacious skies," the class begins again.

Miss Fasola starts to walk back and forth, back and forth, and then, as she gets closer to where I am sitting, I know it's my chance to show off my great voice.

"GOD SHED HIS GRACE ON THEE!" I sing my best.

Miss Prissy Fasola gasps, "It's you, Phoebe Flower. It's you! You are screeching a song that is supposed to make you proud to be an American. You are singing off key and way, way, too loud. Three times today I told the class that a good voice does not have to be a loud voice. March to Dr. Nicely's office right now and I will meet you there after class."

Miss Fasola points to the door. She can't mean me. She's making a mistake. I don't just think I can sing. I know I can sing. I can do anything I want to. I am determined. My dad told me.

"But Miss Fasola," I beg, "how would you ever know I have a great voice if I don't sing loud so that you can hear me? How would you know to pick me to sing the solo all by myself in the second grade concert at the end of the year?"

"Out, Phoebe, out!" Miss Fasola points to the door.

Another Bad Day

This is a mistake. I know it. My dad told me I could do anything I wanted to. I shuffled my feet to the office and muttered under my breath, "Miss Fasola thinks she's so la-di-da."

"Hi, Phoebe," Mrs. Walkerspeaking, the school secretary, greets me. "How's the little heroine doing and why the sad face, Phoebe? That's not a heroine's face."

"Hi, Mrs. Walkerspeaking," I say softly. "I'm having a bad day. Do you ever think you can do something and then find out you can't? Well, my dad said I can do anything I want if I am determined, and I am, but I still can't do it. Miss Fasola says I should be proud to be an American and that I ruined 'America the Beautiful.' She says I sing way, way, off the key. I have to see Dr. Nicely, and I can't sing anymore today because I am too loud. How will Miss Fasola know that I should be the one picked to sing the solo in the second grade concert at the end of the year if I don't sing loud enough for her to hear me? Do you know how to sing, Mrs. Walkerspeaking?"

"You have had a bad day, Phoebe," Mrs. Walkerspeaking says. "Yes, I love to sing. I remember my second grade end-of-the-year concert. Ricky Speck threw up all over my new dress and the smell made me feel sick to my stomach, so I sat down on the bleachers. My mother couldn't see me and thought I had fainted. She came running up to the bleachers screaming my name and trying to find me. The music teacher had to stop the concert and I had to leave the auditorium because I had throw-up all over me, and I smelled. There wasn't a drop of throw-up on Ricky Speck. All the kids were holding their noses, so they couldn't sing! The music teacher told me I ruined the whole concert."

"Really?" I say.

"Really!" answers Mrs. Walkerspeaking. "I'll let Dr. Nicely know that you're here, and don't worry, Phoebe, you have more talents than singing."

It seems like two days before Dr. Nicely opens her door. "Hi, Phoebe. Come on into my office. How are you today? Do you have a problem?"

"Well, Dr. Nicely, as a matter of fact, I do," I say as I get up and walk into her office. "You see, my dad and I had a heart-to-heart talk, and he says I can do anything if I am determined, and I am, but I can't. Miss Fasola says I ruined 'America the Beautiful' because I sing off the key. She says I make every one else ruin it too because I'm too loud. How will she ever know to pick me to sing the solo in the second grade concert at the end of the year if I don't sing loud enough for her to hear me? Did you know Mrs. Walkerspeaking ruined her second grade concert? Can you sing, Dr. Nicely?"

55

"Well, I guess I can, Phoebe, but there are lot of other things I can't do," Dr. Nicely answered. "I can't whistle and I can't ice skate."

"Gee, that's too bad, Dr. Nicely," I tell her. "I am pretty good at both of those things."

"See, Phoebe, we all have special talents," Dr. Nicely smiles, "so please try to sing softer in music class. Miss Fasola is proud of the way her children sing and she believes that a good voice . . ."

". . . does not have to be a loud voice," we both say together and laugh.

"Well, I'll try, Dr. Nicely, but I did promise my dad," I answer.

"Please try, Phoebe, because we don't like to see Miss Fasola angry, do we?" Dr. Nicely asks. "Now, I'll have to write a note home to your mother and you'll have to apologize to Miss Fasola. Maybe you could think of something else to be determined to do. I'm sure your father wouldn't care if you changed your mind."

"OK, I'll try," I say sadly to Dr. Nicely, "but, I really wanted to sing a solo in the second grade concert at the end of the year and hear everyone cheer."

I start to open the door and Dr. Nicely calls, "Cheer up, Phoebe, and remember, a good voice . . ."

". . . doesn't have to be a loud voice," I finish and giggle.

I wish I could rip up this note. I'm sure my mom will find out if I do, and then I'll really be in trouble.

Later that night, while Mom's making dinner and holding Walter in one arm, I give her the note. Maybe, if I'm lucky, she'll put it down and forget to read it.

"Phoebe Flower!" my mother shouts at me from the kitchen. "Why

56

did you get Miss Fasola so angry? You shouldn't be told three times no to sing so loud. Did you forget . . . Miss Fasola is our neighbor? I see her jogging when I walk Buddy Dog. I see her at the grocery store. What am I going to say to her the next time I see her?"

"It's Miss Prissy Fasola, Mom, Miss P. F." I tell her, "and I have an idea . . . maybe you should tell Miss Prissy Fasola that I want to sing a solo all by myself in the second grade concert at the end of the year. I want to see the whole audience stand and clap and cheer."

Amanda bursts out laughing. "Are you kidding?" she says during screams of laughter. "Who told you that you could sing, Phoebe? You are crazy!"

"Please, Amanda, be nice," sighs Mom. "Phoebe's not crazy. She's just a little unsure of herself."

"She sounds pretty sure of herself to me," Amanda answers. "Even I know Gloria Von Kloppenstein will be picked to sing the solo at the end of the year concert and I'm not even in second grade. Gloria sings like an opera singer! Phoebe, you don't!"

"Please, girls," Mom begs, "Grandma Wig is coming for dinner. Let's not tell her about this note and please don't argue in front of her."

"Great idea!" I answer.

"I'll try!" Amanda says with a mean smile.

What Time Is It?

I start to set the table. I can't wait for Grandma Wig to come. She always cheers me up. Sometimes she brings me a little present. But, even if she doesn't, I love her anyway.

"Hi, Mama!" I hear Walter yell as the front door opens.

"Hi, Punkie!" Grandma yells back to Walter.

I run up to Grandma and throw my arms around her waist. "Hi, my sweetie, Phoebe!" she says as she hugs me back. "Something smells very good in here and I'm pretty hungry."

"Dinner is almost ready!" Mom yells from the kitchen. "Phoebe, go upstairs and get Amanda, please."

"Hurry back, Phoebe, I can't wait to hear about your day at school," Grandma Wig says with a smile.

During dinner Grandma tells us about her day at the grocery store and how she saved $.75 on cat food. She tells us about her Bingo game at the senior citizen hall and how some of her friends are getting car phones.

Then, the worst happens.

"So, Phoebe and Amanda, tell me about your day at school," Grandma Wig asks.

I look at my mom. She looks at me.

"Well, Grandma," Amanda starts, "I won my spelling bee today. I was the only one in my class that could spell the word encyclopedia. Then, because I am such a wonderful listener, my teacher picked me to take charge of the room while she went to find the custodian."

"Very good, Amanda, I am proud of you. What a great day you had!" Grandma says.

"Thank you, Grandma Wig," Amanda smiles. "Phoebe, it's your turn to tell Grandma about your day."

"Oh, it was OK. I've had better. I'm line leader this week, though," I say.

"You're only line leader because all the other girls in your class already had their turn, Phoebe. Tell Grandma what happened in music, why don't you?" Amanda smirked.

"Amanda, you promised," says Mom.

"Oops," smiles Amanda, "I guess I forgot."

"What happened, sweetie, Phoebe?" asks Grandma. "You can tell me. I love to hear all about your day, the good and the bad."

"Well, Grandma," I begin, "when I talked to my dad this summer, he told me I could do anything I wanted if I tried hard enough. He said that all I needed was determination and I would be happy. So I thought and I thought about what I wanted to do. I decided I wanted to sing a solo in the second grade concert at the end of the year just like Gloria Von Kloppenstein did in first grade. I want to see the whole audience stand and clap and cheer. But . . . Miss Prissy Fasola said I sing way off the key

and too loud and that I ruined 'America the Beautiful.' How will she
know I can sing if I don't sing loud? That's what I want to know. She
sent me to the office, and she was mad. Mom says she sees Miss Prissy
in the grocery store and now she'll be embarrassed to see her."

"You forgot the part about how she had already warned you three
times," adds Amanda.

"Amanda, please!" sighs Mom.

"Listen, Phoebe," says Grandma Wig, "I always wanted to sing, too,
but I never was very good. How about if you and I think of something

61

else you can be determined to do? Your dad won't care, I'm sure. He just wants you to be happy. We'll think of something after dinner, OK?"

"Why don't you be determined to stay out of trouble for one whole day," Amanda laughs.

After dinner, Grandma sits on the couch and I plop down next to her. She puts her arm around me and we snuggle. "Can you tie your shoe, Phoebe?" she asks me.

"Yeah, I learned how to do that this summer," I tell her.

"Let's see, can you tell time?"

"Well, sort of, I guess. I can read the clock in Mom's bedroom."

"I mean, can you tell time on a real clock or a watch; the clocks that have hands that go around, like the clock in the kitchen?" Grandma asks.

"No, not yet," I tell her.

"Then, that's it, Phoebe. You can be determined to tell time by the end of the school year. That's something you'll feel proud of and so will your dad and mom. I'll be able to help you, and Miss Fasola won't be mad because you won't be singing too loud. What do you think?" Grandma asks again. "We can start tonight."

"Oh, OK," I admit. "Maybe singing wasn't such a great idea."

Grandma teaches me that the small hand tells the hour and the big hand tells the minute, which makes no sense to me. The big hand should tell the hour because it's bigger. She teaches me that when the big hand touches a number it is a five-minute number. Grandma tells me that if I can count by fives, I can figure out the time. I was happy that I could tell her I could count by fives.

The Best Gift Ever

So, for a week I stare at the clock in my classroom and wait for the big hand to touch a number and count by fives and try to remember if it was five after or five before the hour number.

"Phoebe!" Ms. Biz yells at me, "Why are you staring at the clock? Are you going somewhere? Did you finish the two rows of math problems you have to do?"

"Sorry, Ms. Biz, I just didn't want you to forget lunch," I answer her. "You know eating lunch is important for growing children." I couldn't say I was learning how to tell time because lots of kids in my class already know how.

"Phoebe, we already ate lunch. It's two o'clock in the afternoon and you've been staring at the clock all day," Ms. Biz says. "And, I want to see those math problems finished before you go home today because, if they're not finished, you will have a note to take home that says they must be completed for homework tonight."

"Oh yeah, you're right, we did go to lunch, didn't we," I say. "But, Ms. Biz, we didn't go to gym yet, and exercise is important for growing children, too. I just want to make sure you don't forget and I don't mean to be rude, Ms. Biz, but I think it's five after two."

"Thank you, Phoebe, but please pay attention to this math lesson. We don't go to gym for twenty minutes," Ms. Biz reminds me.

Grandma Wig is coming over tonight and I can't wait to show her how I can tell all the five minute times. Sometimes I get the befores and afters mixed up, but I am getting pretty good at it.

When I get home I give my mom the note that says I have to finish my math problems and take them back tomorrow.

"Phoebe, I am disappointed in you," Mom sighs. "Go up to your room and get that math done. Grandma is coming at six o'clock. You have two hours to finish it. Don't plan on going outside until it's done, either."

Yuck! I walk into my bedroom and throw my math book on my bed and watch it bounce up and down. Maybe, if I throw it hard enough, it'll bounce up and out the window. I look out the window and see Robbie playing football with some friends from school. He is so lucky. I grab my nerf football from under my bed and start to toss it up in the air. I can throw a pass so much better than Robbie can. I open my window. "Hey, Robbie! Look up here. Catch this!" I toss the football out the window and it sails right into Robbie's hands.

"Come on out, Phoebe. We need you!" Robbie yells back.

"I will when I finish my math homework," I answer.

"You can do it down here. Watch this!" Robbie bends over and tosses the ball to one of his friends. "Twenty-four, thirty-six, forty-eight, hike!"

"Funny, Robbie," I answer. I sit down and try to do some math, but I hate it. I keep hearing Robbie and the guys playing football. Maybe I'll draw some pictures for Grandma Wig and then do my math.

Next thing I hear is the front door opening. Yea! Grandma Wig is here. I run down the stairs. "Hi, Grandma Wig, it's five minutes after six. You're five minutes late!"

"Phoebe Flower, you sweetie, Phoebe, you! You are the smartest little girl in the world. You learned all that in a week. I am so proud of you!" Grandma Wig laughs.

"I knew that in kindergarten," Amanda yells from the bedroom.

"Hi, Amanda!" Grandma Wig yells back. "You are smart, too. I know that."

"Amanda, come and help me with dinner please," Mom calls. "Did you do your homework, Phoebe?"

"Just about," I tell her.

"Phoebe, will you sit down on the couch with me?" Grandma Wig asks me. "I have something to tell you."

I sit as close as I can to Grandma Wig.

"Phoebe, I have something for you. Your grandfather gave this to me many years ago. It's a very special treasure to me, but I want you to have it." Grandma Wig hands me a velvet box. I open up this velvet box and inside is the most beautiful watch I have ever seen. It's gold and shiny and it looks like something a movie star would wear.

"Grandma Wig!" I gasp, "Is this for me?"

"Yes, Phoebe, it is," Grandma Wig answers. "I thought to myself, 'How's Phoebe supposed to learn to tell time if she doesn't have a watch?' I even had your initials engraved on the back of it. See?"

I turn it over and there, on the back, is 'To P.F., with love.' It's the most beautiful thing I have ever seen. I think I will burst from happiness.

"Grandma Wig," I say, as I wrap my arms hard around her neck, "this is the most special treasure anyone could ever have in their whole life. My heart is going to blow up. I'm so happy. Thank you!"

"You've already said thanks, Phoebe, by starting to learn how to tell time."

At dinner I can hardly eat anything. I can't stop staring at my new watch. Amanda smiles when I show it to her and says, 'Lovely," but when Grandma Wig leaves she says, "Big deal, Phoebe, you'll probably lose it in a week. You can't keep track of anything you own."

Before I take my bath to get ready for bed Mom warns, "Phoebe, did you finish all your homework? You don't have your watch on, do you?"

"Of course not, Mom," I answer, telling the truth for both questions. "I'm as careful with my watch as a mother robin is with her new babies."

When it's time for bed, I check to see if my watch is on my shelf, safe and sound, where I put it before my bath. The next morning all I can think about is showing my watch to Robbie and Elizabeth. I don't like Elizabeth very much and she doesn't like me. I can't wait to put on that watch, march onto that bus and ask Elizabeth if she wants to know what time it is.

Robbie's at the bus stop when I get there. "How come you're so early, Phoebe? You're usually running out the front door with a piece of toast in your mouth."

"Early? Is it early, Robbie? Let me check," I say as I roll up my sleeve. "Yes, you're right. It is early. My new watch that my grandmother gave me that is engraved with my initials P. F. on the back says the bus will be here in five minutes. Want to see it, Robbie?"

'Wow, Phoebe, your grandmother really gave that to you? That's a beauty! You're so lucky! Can you tell time?" Robbie asks me.

"Of course I can. I wouldn't wear a watch if I couldn't, silly," I tell him.

When the bus pulls up, I race up the stairs and jump into the seat next to Elizabeth. "Guess what time it is, Elizabeth?" I ask. "Who cares?" Elizabeth answers me.

"Everybody cares what time it is, Elizabeth. I have a watch my grandmother gave me with my initials P.F. engraved on the back. It's a very special treasure because it used to be hers. Want to see it?"

"Not really. I have a watch too. It has Mickey Mouse on it and I got mine at Disney World," Elizabeth brags.

"Are your initials on the back?" I grin.

"Big deal," Elizabeth says and turns her head to look out the window. I know she wishes she had a watch like mine.

My Initials -
Your Initials

When I get to school, I stop by Mrs. Ward's room to show her my new watch. "Your watch is so pretty, Phoebe. Be careful not to lose it. Your grandmother must love you very much to give you a watch like that."

"I'm as careful with this watch as a mother robin is with her baby birds," I tell Mrs. Ward. "It's a very special treasure, you know."

Ms. Biz lets me show my watch for "show and tell." I tell the class that my initials, P.F., are engraved on the back. "How can your initials be P.F. if both Phoebe and Flower start with the 'F' sound, Phoebe?" Gloria asks.

"Good question, Gloria," Ms. Biz answers. "When a P and an H are together they make the 'F' sound. Phoebe starts that way and so do phone and Philip. This is a good learning experience for us, Phoebe. Thank you!"

I smile.

Then Ms. Biz gives me a message to take to the office because she

68

knows I want to show my watch to Mrs. Walkerspeaking. "Hey, Mrs. Walkerspeaking, do you know what time it is?

"No, Phoebe, what time is it?" she asks me.

"It's five minutes to ten o'clock. What do you think of that?" I ask her.

"That is a very good time, Phoebe. Thanks!" Mrs. Walkerspeaking answers.

All day long I have to remind Ms. Biz what time it is. She says, "Thank you very much, Phoebe, but could you do some school work? I want to see your homework on my desk from yesterday before you go home today." I am too excited to do school work, so I look at my watch and practice telling time.

When we go to music, Miss Fasola asks me, "Phoebe, why are you looking at your wrist today and not singing? Last week, I asked you not to sing so loudly. I didn't mean for you to not sing at all."

"Don't you know, Miss Prissy Fasola," Elizabeth yells out, "Phoebe has a very special treasure. The whole wide world knows Phoebe got a new watch."

"Yes, I did," I answer, proudly, "and it has my initials, P.F., right on the back. The same initials that you have, Miss Prissy Fasola. Want me to show you my initials?"

"Don't take it off, Phoebe. You'll lose it," she tells me. "I believe you."

All day long I tell everyone I see what time it is. I love my new watch. I don't even mind being in school. I know when it's time to go home without anyone telling me. I can't wait to write my dad and tell him about my new watch. He'll be so happy and proud of me.

I jump on the school bus, "Hi, Mike!" I greet the bus driver, "Do you know that it is almost ten minutes after three? You are right on time today. Good job!"

70

"Thanks, Phoebe," Mike smiles.

"Almost ten after three?" Elizabeth asks, as I sit down, "Don't you know exactly what time that is? What good is a new watch if you can't read it?"

"Of course, I know, Elizabeth. I just didn't want to make Mike nervous and think he was late," I answer, thinking that I better call Grandma Wig and ask her how to tell time EXACTLY.

When Robbie and I get off the bus, I see the mail truck coming down the street. I decide to wait and tell Bill, the mailman, that he is right on time today. I just love this watch. I roll up my sleeve and giggle when I see this beautiful gold watch that is mine, all mine.

"Hi Bill!" I yell, "I just want you to know you're right on time today. It's three thirty! You're doing a great job!"

"Hey, Phoebe, look up!" Robbie calls from his front yard, "catch this!"

I turn around and see a football heading straight toward my head. I duck fast. The football zooms past me, through the mail truck window and into Bill's bag of mail.

"So sorry, Bill, I'll get it." I run over to the truck, reach my hands into the mailbag moving letters and magazines and pull out the ball.

"I guess Robbie needs to practice his passing, doesn't he?" Bill grins.

"Maybe he thought he was playing basketball," I laugh.

"Bye, Phoebe, stay out of trouble," Bill yells as I skip-hop into my house.

"Listen carefully, girls. We have to eat dinner early because I have to stop at the drugstore before we go to Amanda's dance lessons. So, do your homework and then help set the table. Can one of you play with Walter while I cook dinner?"

"I'll play with Walter," I volunteer.

"Phoebe, first, I have to talk to you," Mom says in an angry voice. "Ms. Biz called me today and said that you did not have your homework done today. I am putting my foot down once and for all. If you don't get your work done in school you will not be allowed out of this house for one whole week unless it's to go to school. Do you understand that? I really mean business, Phoebe. Now go upstairs and get your homework done so we can eat and go to dance lessons. Amanda will play with Walter."

This time I can tell Mom really means it. I go upstairs and lock myself in the bathroom to do my homework. I only have six more problems to go when my mother calls, "Phoebe Flower, time to eat!"

The rest of the night is crazy! We get a flat tire on the way home from dance lessons. Mom reads us our bedtime story while we are in the bathtub. Amanda can't find one of her red shoes that she insists on wearing to school tomorrow, so we all have to hunt for that.

Lost, But Not Found

All night long I dream about bars on my window and guards standing at the front and back door of my house so I can't sneak out. When I wake up the next morning, I'm thinking about how I can finish those six problems before it's time for math. Maybe Robbie can help me.

"Hey, Robbie!" I yell as I cross the street to wait for the school bus. "I need your help! You've got to save me."

"Let me guess, Phoebe. You lost your watch," Robbie says.

I freeze! I reach for my wrist and feel my whole body getting hot. My legs start to shake. There is no watch. The watch is not on my wrist. I grab the other wrist. It's not there, either. I start shaking and screaming, "ROBBIE, HELP!! My watch is gone. Where do you think it is?"

"Gee, Phoebe, I don't know, but you better get out of the road. You're going to get hit by a car."

"Hit by a car? Is that all you can think of ? My watch is gone, my watch that is a very special treasure and has my initials on the back that my grandmother gave me that my grandfather gave her. I have to find my watch." I sob and move out of the road.

"Here comes the bus, Phoebe. Just think about where you wore it last," Robbie says trying to help me. "We'll find it!"

I drag my feet up the stairs of the school bus thinking about what Robbie said. Where did I wear it last? That is the big question. I can't think. My brain isn't working. All I can think about is my Grandma's sad face when she finds out I lost that watch. Everybody thought I'd lose it and now I did. There is no way I can let anybody know I lost it.

"Don't sit next to me, Phoebe, if you're going to tell me what time it is every second," Elizabeth warns me.

I don't say a word. I walk past Elizabeth and find a seat by myself. I have to think. I have to think hard. I remember! I showed it for "show and tell." I jump out of my seat as soon as the bus slows down. "Phoebe Flower," the bus driver yells, "stay in your seat until the bus stops!"

I walk the fast walk down the hall to my classroom. Ms. Biz is writing on the chalkboard. "Hi, Phoebe, you're the first one here today. You're usually last. Did you run?"

"Oh no, Ms. Biz, I walked the fast walk. Can I ask you something?"

"Sure, Phoebe, what is it?" Ms. Biz asks me.

"Did you find anything yesterday in the classroom that shouldn't be here after all the kids left to go home?"

"I don't understand what you're asking. What should I have found?"

"Well, you know, if somebody lost something and they couldn't find it and then you saw something that you thought shouldn't be just laying around in a classroom after all the kids were gone . . ." I tried to explain.

I begin to hear the rest of the kids coming in the door.

74

"Did you lose something, Phoebe?" Ms. Biz asks.

"I'm not really sure if I did or didn't, but if I did, please, Ms. Biz, did you find it?" I take a deep breath and close my eyes.

"Oh, I understand, Phoebe. No, I'm sorry I didn't, but, if you want to check Lost and Found, why don't you go to the office? Good luck!" Ms. Biz gives me a hug.

"Good idea," I think, and hurry off to ask Mrs. Walkerspeaking.

It's kind of busy in the office, but I wiggle through all the adults. I say, "Excuse me, excuse me, this is an emergency." Everyone probably thinks I'm going to throw up so they move aside. I finally get to Mrs. Walkerspeaking's desk and tap her on the shoulder.

"Mrs. Walkerspeaking, I need your help. Is anything in the Lost and Found box that shouldn't be there?" I ask, huffing and puffing from squeezing through the crowd.

"Yes, Phoebe, everything in the Lost and Found box shouldn't be there," she giggles.

"That was funny, Mrs. Walkerspeaking, but this is sort of an emergency. Someone has lost something that is very special and it shouldn't be lost. Can I look in the Lost and Found box, please?"

"Sure, Phoebe, but I don't think what you're looking for is there. No one has turned in anything in two days except an old chewed up pencil and I doubt you're looking for that. Oh no!" Mrs. Walkerspeaking gasps, "You didn't lose the watch your grandmother gave you?"

Tears start to fill my eyes.

"Have you asked Ms. Biz? Did you check with Mr. Gordon, the custodian? Did you have Art, Music or Gym yesterday? Did you ask the bus driver?" Mrs. Walkerspeaking asks, almost out of breath.

"Yes, no, yes, music, and no." I try to answer all at once.

"Well, Phoebe, first, I'd ask Mr. Gordon, and then, I'd ask your bus driver. You'll have to wait to ask Miss Prissy Fasola. She called in sick with the flu, and I don't think she'll be back for a few days. Good luck, Phoebe, and don't worry, you'll find it." Mrs. Walkerspeaking squeezes my hand.

I leave the office and go to find Mr. Gordon. As I walk past the broom closet, I hear, "Pssst!" Robbie's sticks his head out the door and holds up his magnifying glass to show me. "Don't look in here, Phoebe," Robbie whispers, "I've already searched it out and there is no evidence of a watch. Don't worry, Phoebe, we'll find it." Robbie always makes me smile.

I find Mr. Gordon and he says he hasn't seen anything gold and shiny with initials on the back, but he'd let me know if he did. The rest of the day I do nothing but think about where that beautiful watch could be. Ms. Biz must feel sorry for me because she doesn't call on me at all. She doesn't even ask if I have my homework finished. When it is time to go home, I try to be the first one on the bus so I can ask Mike if he found it. "Nothing was turned in, Phoebe," Mike tells me, "but I will check all the seats carefully when the kids get off the bus."

"You're the best, Mike!" I tell him.

Vacuum Disaster

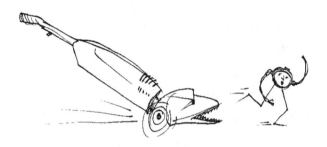

Robbie gets on the bus and sits next to me. "Hey, Phoebe, any luck finding you-know-what?"

"None!" I answer. I tell him where I looked.

"Want me to come over to your house and help you search? I don't have much homework. If you're really feeling brave, we could always go to Miss Prissy Fasola's house and then you wouldn't have to wait two days to ask her," Robbie says.

"Wow, you are a good friend, Robbie. I don't even like to talk to Miss Prissy when she feels good. Think about what a grouch she must be when she has the flu. It's a scary thought." We both laugh. "Thanks for offering to help, but I don't want anyone in my family to even guess I lost the watch. Amanda might think it's weird if we're both looking under tables and chairs.

When I get home, I try to act normal so no one will notice me. "Hello, Mother, hello, Walter," I say. I hang up my coat and put away my book bag and have a snack. Amanda is still at cheerleading practice, so this is a great time to look for my watch.

"Phoebe, what's wrong with you?" my mother asks.

"Wrong? Why do you say wrong?" I answer my mother.

"Well, for one thing you hung up your coat and put away your book bag, which you never do, and the next thing is you walked right past the brand new vacuum I bought today and you didn't notice it. Remember my old one? It wouldn't pick up air. This one works perfectly. I vacuumed all day. I vacuumed the whole house. This new vacuum is so strong, I think it could vacuum up our car," Mom laughs. I want to cry.

I go to my room, close the door, and put the pillow over my head. There is no use looking. I'm sure my mother vacuumed it up. I tell Mom I'm sick and can't come down to dinner.

When I wake up, Mom is feeling my forehead. "Phoebe, are you OK? It's morning and you slept through the night. Is something bothering you?"

"No, everything's fine. It's just . . . ah . . . " I start to tell her.

"Did you ever find my red shoe?" Amanda asks as she opens my door.

"It's late, Mom," I say as I jump out of bed, "I better get ready for school."

Today is worse than yesterday. I have no more ideas where to look for that beautiful, shiny special watch. Ms. Biz doesn't feel sorry for me anymore. She calls on me twice. At least she doesn't send home another note. Robbie tries to cheer me up by telling me jokes. I pretend to laugh so he feels better. When I get home from school, I am sadder than I was when I left. How will I ever go to school tomorrow?

Mom is waiting for me when I come in the house, "Great news, Phoebe.

79

I've got something to cheer you up. Guess who's coming for dinner?"

Mom doesn't realize the only thing that would cheer me up is if our new vacuum got the flu and threw up my watch.

"Who?" I ask.

"Your favorite person in the whole world."

"Grandma Wig!" I scream. "No, not tonight, Mom. You must be joking!"

"Phoebe Flower, you love Grandma Wig. What is wrong with you?" Mom looks shocked.

"She can't come tonight, Mom. I think I'm getting sick. You don't want her to catch it, do you?"

"Phoebe, you are not getting sick and Grandma Wig is coming, so you better change your attitude very quickly. Now go upstairs and do your homework so you can visit with her," Mom says angrily.

I go upstairs to do my homework. Amanda pops open her door and says with a smile, "I agree with you this time, Phoebe. I think you are sick . . . sick in the head."

I run to my bedroom and slam the door. How will I ever keep Grandma Wig from asking me what time it is? Once Amanda discovers I don't want to talk about it, she'll find out I lost the watch.

I hear the phone ringing. Maybe Grandma Wig is calling to say she can't come.

Now That's
a Great Idea!

"PHOEBE!" My mom is calling my name.

I open my bedroom door.

"The telephone is for you, Phoebe," Mom yells.

It's probably Robbie with another joke. "Hello!" I say.

"Hello, is this Phoebe Flower?" the voice asks.

"Yep, who is this?" I answer.

"Well, Phoebe, this is Miss Prissy Fasola and I think I have something that belongs to you."

"WHO did you say this is?" I ask.

" I said . . . this is Miss Prissy FASOLA! Do you want me to sing it to you? I went to my mailbox today and found an envelope from Bill, the mailman. I will read you the note that was inside.

Dear Miss Fasola,

Yesterday, I found a woman's watch in the bottom of my mailbag. I have no idea how it got there, but it has your initials on it, so I decided it must be yours.

Sincerely,

Bill

Well, Phoebe, it is not my watch and I remember two days ago you were telling everyone in the school the time, and I thought it just might be yours."

"Miss Fasola, it IS my watch! Do you really have my very special treasure? Can I come to your house right now and get it, please? You are so wonderful, Miss Prissy Fasola. Just now I was thinking my life was over. You have saved my grandmother from being sad. You have saved my life. Thank you, thank you, thank you."

I slam down the phone without waiting for Miss Fasola to answer me. I run down the stairs and out the front door and yell to my mother that I will be right back.

"Where are you going?" my mother calls as I run as fast as I can to Robbie's house. I knock and Robbie comes to the front door. I grab his arm and pull him down the street by his shirtsleeve. "Where are we going?" he yells.

"To Miss Fasola's house." I try to sound calm.

"You must be kidding, Phoebe. You're just one big kidder. Tell me you're kidding. There is no way you'd go there," Robbie pants as we run.

"She's got my watch, Robbie. We have to." I start to get a funny feeling in my stomach as we get closer to Miss Fasola's house. I've never been to a teacher's house before.

83

I run up the porch stairs and ring the doorbell twice. Robbie hides underneath the front porch.

The door opens—"Ah, ah, ah, Miss Prissy Fasola," I pant out of breath, "I'm Phoebe Flower. We have the same initials."

"I know who you are, Phoebe, I called you, remember?" Miss Fasola was dressed in a long pink bathrobe. She looked sick.

"Come in Phoebe. You, too, Robbie. You must be uncomfortable under the porch. I'll go get your watch. It's upstairs in my jewelry box where a watch should be when it's not being worn." Miss Fasola's phone rings. "Come inside, both of you. I won't bite. Wait here. I have to answer the phone, first."

Robbie and I look at each other. Robbie is shaking. We step inside to wait. Hurry up, Miss Fasola, I think to myself. Don't take too long. We could hear her talking on the upstairs phone. Did she forget we were waiting?

Then I see it! In the corner of the living room is a very big, no, an enormous, black, shiny piano—bigger than even a car. I nudge Robbie and point to it. He just stands there, not moving an inch. "Maybe," I whisper to him, "I'll just tip-toe run over to that shiny piano so I can take a closer look. I've never seen anything so big."

Robbie's eyes open like saucers. "Are you a complete nut? Do you want to die? Stay right here, Phoebe."

I look up the stairs. I don't hear Miss Fasola coming. I tiptoe run over to the piano as quietly as I can. Those white piano keys are smiling at me like shiny white teeth. I have to touch them. They feel so cool and smooth.

"PHOEBE FLOWER, WHAT ARE DOING?" I feel two hands pressing on my shoulders.

84

"Oh, I'm so sorry, Miss Fasola. I didn't mean to touch it. I just couldn't help it."

"Don't be sorry, Phoebe. I mean, what are you doing playing the piano? Who taught you to play? Do you know you are playing 'Mary Had A Little Lamb'? Do you take piano lessons?"

"No, I just figured it out. Doesn't everybody know how to do that?" I say.

"No, everybody doesn't know how. Come on over and listen to Phoebe play, Robbie. I think I have a wonderful idea!"

Miss Fasola tells us her idea.

We skip-run all the way back. When we get to Robbie's house, we slap each other a high-five. It's been a wonderful day—the best day ever! "You are the greatest friend in the whole world. Thanks for helping me find my lost treasure, Robbie!" I tell him as I look at my watch.

I run to my house and burst open my front door.

"Where have you been?" Mom calls to me from the kitchen, "We've been worried."

"Grandma Wig, Mom, Amanda, Walter, Buddy Dog, do you want to know what time it is?" I shout.

"Sure, Phoebe! What time is it?" Grandma Wig answers.

"It's time for me to be determined to play a PIANO solo all by myself in the second grade concert at the end of the year. Miss Prissy Fasola says if I practice long enough and hard enough I will see the whole audience stand and clap and cheer."

Grandma Wig walks over to me, puts her arms around me. I close my eyes. I feel so good. Grandma makes me *sure* I can do it. That's what hugs are for.

Part 3

That's What
Friends Are For

Introducing
... the One, the Only
... Gloria

Things are better now that I'm third grade. First of all, it's not second grade, so that means I am closer to being out of school forever. Second of all, I have Mr. Blister, the only man teacher in the school. Everybody wanted him for a teacher! Third of all, and most fabulous of all, I have a best friend! I have never had a best friend before. I don't think I can count Robbie. He's like my brother. He only acts like my friend when we play alone. If his friends ask him to play football, he won't let me go with him even though he knows I can zigzag run faster than any of the boys. He doesn't like to do girl stuff, either, like talk on the phone when he's doing his homework. And, when I sit next to him on the bus and I want to tell him a secret, he won't let me lean close to him and whisper it in his ear. I say, "Robbie, if you want to hear this, you better let me sit close and whisper it in your ear."

Robbie always says, "Shh, Phoebe! Get away from me."

My best friend's name is Gloria Von Kloppenstein. She sang the solo in the first grade concert. She also sang the solo in the second grade concert and I, Phoebe Flower, played the piano while she sang. The audience clapped and cheered for both of us.

Miss Prissy Fasola, the music teacher at my school, told me that, if I wanted to learn to play the piano for the second grade concert, I would have to practice, practice, practice. She said I could stay after school and she would help me. Miss Fasola said that sometimes Gloria Von Kloppenstein could stay too, and we would practice together.

When I first thought about practicing with Gloria, I thought, "YUCK!" I never liked her. I wanted to be the one to sing the solo. So, the first day we stayed after school to practice together, I said (just to make Gloria mad), "This will be so much fun won't it, Gloria Von Clappenstein?" Gloria laughed so hard and so long I thought she would choke. After that, we became best friends. Gloria said, "Phoebe, you are the funniest person I have ever known."

Gloria isn't funny at all, but, boy, can she laugh! Whenever Gloria is sad I always say, "Gloria, what's the difference between an orange and a matta baby?" "What's a matta baby?" Gloria asks. "Nothing, baby, what's a matta with you?" I answer her. Gloria laughs and laughs even though she has heard that joke a thousand times.

Gloria gets straight A's in school and she always sits up straight and raises her hand when she wants to talk. She's pretty and smart and she wears the coolest clothes. She is very quiet and never gets yelled at for talking too much or for getting out of her seat to get a drink of water when she's not supposed to. Gloria doesn't have untied shoelaces that look like dirty spaghetti, either.

Gloria lives with her father and her older brother. Her mother died when she was two years old. I asked her once if she missed her mother and Gloria said, "Yeah, I miss her, I guess. I only remember a little bit about her, but my dad is really nice. He makes the best chocolate chip cookies in the whole wide world. He sometimes reads me two books a day and he takes me to the movies every single month. Maybe you could go with us sometime, Phoebe. "I would love to, Gloria! I've never been to the movies with a friend before," I told her.

One night, when we were sitting at the dinner table, I asked my mom if I could invite Gloria over to play.

"Gloria, the girl who sang the solo in the first grade concert?" Amanda asked.

"Yes, that's the Gloria I mean; the one, the only, Gloria Von Kloppenstein! She's my best friend," I said.

"You must be kidding! Why would Gloria want to be your best friend? She could be anybody's best friend. Give me one good reason, Phoebe. Is this some kind of a joke, Mom?" Amanda asked in a mean voice.

"Of course you can invite Gloria over, Phoebe," Mom answered, "and, Amanda, it is no joke. I can think of one million reasons why Gloria would want to be Phoebe's friend. First of all, and best of all, Phoebe is kind. Now, could you try to be kinder to your sister, please?"

"I guess I can try," Amanda answered.

"How about tomorrow?" I asked my mom. "Gloria can ride home from school with me on the bus. We can play in my tree house and jump rope and she can stay for dinner and we can watch TV. Then Gloria can stay overnight. We'll tell ghost stories and we can ride the bus back to school in the morning. How's that for a great idea?"

"Be careful, Mom," Amanda warned, "next thing you know, Phoebe will want us to buy a bigger house so that Gloria can move in."

"Slow down, Phoebe," Mom said. "Gloria can come tomorrow

because I don't have to work, but just to play and stay for dinner. You'll have to do your homework before you play, too."

"Thank you, oh wonderful mother of mine!" I yelled.

"Call her and see if her father says it's okay," Mom told me, "and, while you're at it, call your own father, too. You haven't called him in a week."

"I called Dad yesterday, Mom, and he said he loved hearing from me," Amanda bragged.

"Oh, sure, Mom, I'll call Dad. I know Gloria's father will say 'okay,' though. He's the greatest dad. He makes the best chocolate chip cookies in the whole world," I told Mom.

Gloria's father said she could come home on the bus with me and that he would pick her up at 7:00, after dinner. I couldn't sleep all night. This was going to be the best time ever. I started thinking about what we'd do. We were going to have so much fun.

The next day in school seemed like the longest day of my life. When the bell finally rang for us to get on the bus to go home, I grabbed Gloria's hand and led her to my bus and pushed all the way to the back to find a seat. "Hi, Robbie, this is Gloria Von Kloppenstein. She's my best friend and she is coming over to my house today to play and eat dinner."

"I know Gloria, Phoebe. She's in my class too. Remember?" Robbie said and turned to look out the bus window.

"I think Robbie's jealous of you," I whispered in Gloria's ear.

Gloria moved to sit closer to me.

92

Rolling Meatballs

When we got to my house, I pulled Gloria up the sidewalk to the front door. Buddy Dog came bounding out from behind the bushes and started to sniff and lick Gloria. "Do you like dogs, Gloria?" I asked her. "Buddy Dog won't hurt you. He just likes to sniff and lick."

"I don't have a dog, but I'd love to have one," Gloria answered as she reached down and petted Buddy Dog on the head.

"Come on inside and meet Walter and Pam," I said. "Amanda is at cheerleading practice, lucky for us. She thinks she is the boss of the universe. She's my big sister and she's a real pain, if you know what I mean."

Walter was sitting in his high chair eating Cheerios. "Hi, Walter, this is Gloria. Can you say Gloria?" I asked Walter.

"Oreo!" Walter said.

Gloria laughed out loud.

"Hi, Pam," I said to my mother. "I would like you to meet Gloria Von

94

Kloppenstein, my best friend."

My mother turned around from the sink and glared at me with one eyebrow pushed up to her forehead. "Hi, Gloria, I'm Mrs. Flower. It's very nice to meet you. Oh, and by the way, Phoebe, just in case you forgot, I'm 'Mom' to you."

"Oh, I didn't forget, Pam, oops, sorry, I mean, Mom. I just wanted Gloria to know your real name. Maybe she'll want to write you a letter some day." I smiled and Gloria giggled.

"Why don't you girls go out and play and I'll call you when dinner's ready. You can do your homework after dinner. How's that for a good idea, Phoebe?" Mom said.

"Great idea, Mom, but first we have to go upstairs and put on play clothes. I don't want to get my outfit all grass-stained. You know how careful I am."

"No, I don't know how careful you are, but that's a very good idea," Mom answered.

I grabbed Gloria's hand and dragged her up the stairs toward my bedroom.

"Come on, Gloria, we have to hurry," I whispered to her. "We have to sneak into Amanda's room while she's at cheerleading practice. She'll kill me if she knows I'm in her room. She has the neatest stuff."

I pushed open Amanda's door and pointed to the sign that says "KEEP OUT!". Before Gloria knew what I was doing, I pulled open Amanda's closet doors and wiggled inside her closet, past her shoes to the way back corner. "Ah, I found it," I thought to myself. I crawled backwards out of her closet and placed the box I found on Amanda's bed.

"What's in there?" Gloria asked.

"Just wait and see," I told Gloria.

"Wow!" Gloria gasped when I opened the box. "This is so cool. She's got a diary in here. I always wanted one of those. She's even got lipstick and blush and eye shadow."

"What color lipstick is it, Gloria?" I asked. "I wonder if it will go with my tee shirt."

"It's called 'Bubble Gum'," Gloria answered. "Won't Amanda be mad if you put on her lipstick?"

"Sure, she'll be mad, if she finds out," I said as I put on the lipstick. "Amanda is mad all the time, anyway, but she won't find out. Amanda never really notices me. She only thinks about herself."

"Phoebe, I can hear your mother talking to someone and I didn't hear the phone ring. Do you think Amanda's home from practice?" Gloria seemed nervous.

"Yikes, that does sound like her voice! We better get out of here. Hand me the diary and lipstick, Gloria. I don't want you killed the first time you come to visit me." I grabbed the box and threw it in the back of the closet. I took Gloria's hand and we ran down the hall to my room and closed the door behind us.

"Whew! That was a close one!" I said, huffing and puffing.

Mom made spaghetti and meatballs for dinner and Gloria said it was her favorite thing to eat in the whole world. Amanda told us she was sure she would be picked to be captain of the cheerleading team because her coach told her that she jumped higher than a kangaroo.

"I would love to cheerlead when I get older," Gloria said.

"Maybe I can teach you some cheers after dinner, Gloria," Amanda offered.

"That's okay, Amanda," I said, "Gloria and I have to go to the tree house after dinner and spy on Robbie and his friends. Maybe next time."

"But I really would love to learn some cheers, Amanda. Maybe we'll have time for one," Gloria smiled.

"Phoebe, you look flushed and your lips look very red today. Are you feeling all right?" my mother asked.

"Never felt better, Mom," I answered.

"Yes, your lips look pinkish. Mom's right. Do you have lipstick on, Phoebe?" Amanda stared at me.

"Now where in the world would I get lipstick, Amanda? You're so silly. It must be the spaghetti sauce." I quickly grabbed my fork and picked up a big meatball covered with sauce and shoved into my mouth. I did this so fast that I hit another meatball on my plate. It rolled off the table and splattered onto the floor.

"Oh that was just great, Phoebe!" Amanda said, "Now clean it up."

"Ball, ball," Walter giggled.

"I'll clean it up," my mother said. "Please try to be more careful, Phoebe."

Gloria took one look at me and started laughing so hard she made snorting noises through her nose. She asked to be excused. When she returned she apologized for laughing so hard.

"It wasn't your fault, Gloria, Phoebe is just clumsy," Amanda said." So, the next time you come over, maybe I'll teach you to cheer and you and I can sing some songs together. I sang a solo once in third grade."

"It was only two words, Amanda. I wouldn't really call that a solo. Plus, the next time Gloria comes over we are going to jump rope and use my new jewelry-making kit, right, Gloria?" I asked.

"Sure, Phoebe, but I'll have time to sing, too." Gloria smiled at Amanda.

"Eat your salad, Phoebe," mom said. "You haven't touched it."

I shoved some salad into my mouth, wishing Amanda would disappear. A piece of lettuce fell off my plate to the floor. I was sure no one saw it fall. I quickly ducked my head under the table to find the piece of lettuce. Then carefully, I grabbed it between two toes on my right foot and gently lifted it. I thought this was pretty clever, so I lifted it with my toes up to the table and placed the lettuce back on my salad plate.

Gloria started to giggle. Amanda shook her head. Walter stared at my salad plate.

"Phoebe Flower, what are you doing?" Her face was very red. "Come into the living room. I have to speak to you now."

"But, Mom," I started.

My mother walked into the living room, turned around to face me. She took her right pointer finger, pointed it to the ground and drew an invisible line. "Do you see this?" she asked.

"What?" I answered.

"The line I just drew with my finger," she answered.

"Yes," I said, but I didn't really see it since it was invisible.

"Well, you have crossed that line, Phoebe Flower. I am angry and you will never ever have another friend over to this house if you don't stop showing off. Do you understand what I am saying?"

"Yes," I gulped.

"Now go in there and finish eating and remember your manners. Use your fork, not your toes!"

All Work and
Still No Play

Today when I get to school there's a note on my desk that says:

Dear Phoebe,
I had the best time of my whole life
at your house yesterday.
Thanks so much for inviting me.
                    Love,
                    Your best friend,
                    Gloria

I don't think I've ever been as happy in my whole life. I want to do cartwheels all around the room. Instead, I look over at Gloria and smile so wide I think the corners of my lips are touching my ears.

"Good morning, boys and girls," says Mr. Blister. "I have a surprise for you today. I'll see if you can guess what it is after I take attendance."

"Robbie," calls Mr. Blister.

"Here!" replies Robbie.

"Isaiah!"

"Here, too!" says Isaiah.

"Elizabeth!"

"Present, Mr. Blister," answers Elizabeth.

"Phoebe!" calls Mr. Blister, ignoring Elizabeth's movie star voice.

"Here!" I reply, smiling at Gloria. I'm so glad we have the same teacher.

Mr. Blister reads on down his list. "Jooling!"

Every head in the classroom turns toward the window side of the room where Mr. Blister is looking. Jooling has hair the color of that delicious black licorice from Fagan's drugstore. It's long and thick and covers part of her eye. Jooling doesn't even look like she heard Mr. Blister call her name.

Getting no reply, Mr. Blister gently asks, "Jooling, are you here? Say 'here,' dear!"

Some of the kids in the class start to giggle.

"Jooling is from Korea, boys and girls, and she is the surprise," Mr. Blister explains. "She doesn't speak very much English, but Jooling is very smart. Her mom and dad are studying to become doctors in the United States. Please show her what good friends you can be."

Mr. Blister continues to take attendance.

The rest of the morning, Jooling sits and stares at her desk. I know this because I usually stare out the window and watch the UPS truck deliver packages to the school. At lunch time I remember what Mr. Blister said about being a good friend.

"Gloria, let's ask Jooling to sit with us at lunch," I say.

"Come on, Phoebe," Gloria answers. "Don't you just want it to be you and me."

"Yeah, but she looks so lonely. Let's just ask her," I say.

101

"Oh, okay!" Gloria agrees.

We both walk over to Jooling's desk. "Hey, Jooling, wanna eat lunch with us?" Gloria asks.

Jooling doesn't even blink her eyes.

"Come on, WE WILL SH—OW YOU THE CAF-E-TER-I-A," I say and stretch out each syllable.

Jooling doesn't move.

"Leave her alone," Gloria says. "She doesn't want to come with us."

Gloria takes my hand and we walk to the cafeteria together.

I love being Gloria's best friend, but it makes schoolwork and homework harder to do. I'm always trying to think of fun things that Gloria and I can do together so that Gloria will keep liking me. Mr. Blister gives us lots of homework, too. Tonight we have to do two pages of math, study twenty-five spelling words and think about the essay we have to write entitled, "What I Am Most Thankful For." Mr. Blister calls on me a lot, too. He says, "Phoebe, you are as flighty as a bumble bee. Try to focus on what we're doing in the classroom." I like him, but he's really not as great as I thought.

Today on the way home from school, I ask Robbie what he's most thankful for. "No way, Phoebe, I'm not telling you that. I don't want you copying my idea and using it for the essay," Robbie says.

"Not this time, Robbie. I know what I'm most thankful for already," I say with a smile, thinking about how I can ask my mom if Gloria can come over on Saturday.

When I walk in the house, Mom is standing at the sink doing the dishes and Walter is sitting in his high chair rubbing crackers in his hair. "Hi, Phoebe, how was your day?" Mom asks with a sigh.

"Just great, Mom," I answer. "Is something wrong?"

"No, I'm just tired, that's all," Mom answers.

"I'll help you, Mom. I can do the vacuuming and dusting and I can fold the clothes, too," I tell her.

"Well, I could use a little help, but if you have homework, that comes first. I am looking forward to an excellent parent conference this month, Phoebe," my mom says.

"Just a tiny bit of homework, Mom. Don't worry about the parent conference. Mr. Blister loves me," I say.

That night at bedtime, when Mom tucks me into bed, she thanks me for all the cleaning I did for her. "You are such a kind little girl, Phoebe."

"Thanks, Mom. Do you think it would be okay if Gloria came over on Saturday?" I ask her.

"Phoebe, that's five days from now," Mom says, "but, I guess so. You did help me a lot today and Gloria seems like such a nice girl."

The next day in school, I can't wait to tell Gloria the good news. She seems very happy and asks me if Amanda will be home. I think she wants it to be just the two of us.

Mr. Blister seems very unhappy with me because I never had enough time to do my homework last night. I told him I had to help my mom because she wasn't feeling well. He said this time he'd let it go, but the next time he would need a note from home explaining why I couldn't finish my homework. He also said I'd have to do last night's and tonight's homework and hand it in tomorrow.

On the way home from school, I hop on the school bus, push in and sit next to Robbie. "Hey, Robbie, wanna play this afternoon and do some homework together?" I ask. "We haven't played together in a long time."

"Yes, I'll help you with your homework, Phoebe, but you'd better come over to my house because I don't want your mother to get mad at me if she finds out," Robbie says.

"You're the best fr—," I start to say. Then I do say, "You're the smartest, Robbie!"

Robbie and I sit on his picnic table. He does my math. I just have to write down the problems and the answers. I should think about writing my essay, but I'd rather think about having fun with Gloria.

"I don't get you, Phoebe," Robbie says. "You don't make any sense. You can add up in your head the prices of all the candy and junk we buy at the store. Then, when we put stuff back, you subtract that and you still know exactly how much it all costs. You argue with the checkout man and you are always right. You come up with the best ideas for your essays, but you never write them. You know how to fix my bike better than my dad does, and you easily figure out how to get into the garage if it's locked. So why are you always getting in trouble with Mr. Blister?"

"I don't get me either, Robbie," I sigh.

Cursive
Catsup

The next day in school, Mr. Blister is thrilled that I have all my math homework done. He even says, "Good job, Phoebe!" and pats me on the head like I pat Buddy Dog. But then, the worst happens! Mr. Blister tells us to take out our pencils for a spelling test.

After the test, Mr. Blister calls me up to his desk. "Phoebe, I know you didn't study these words. In fact I don't think you even looked at them. I'm going to send a note home to your mother telling her that you have to be more responsible with your homework. I want it signed and back by tomorrow. Do you understand?"

"Please, please, no, Mr. Blister! My mom will be so mad at me," I cry.

"Phoebe, your mother and I care about you," Mr. Blister says as he picks up his pen and starts to write.

Mom *is* mad! She says there is no way Gloria can come over on Saturday and that I'd be lucky if I ever had a friend over the rest of my life. I tell her it's just stupid old spelling and that's what dictionaries are for, but she doesn't care. Saturday there is no TV, no phone and no Gloria.

On Monday, when I get to school, I run through the halls to my classroom and find Gloria. "Hi, best friend in the whole world. Sorry that you couldn't come over Saturday. My mom overreacted about my homework. She's fine now." I smile at Gloria. Gloria smiles back.

"It's time to take attendance. Take your seats, please." Mr. Blister claps his hands. "I also have an announcement to make. We have a very good friend in this classroom. I was told that Gloria Von Kloppenstein took our new girl, Jooling, to the movies on Saturday. Is this correct, Gloria?"

"That's right, Mr. Blister, and we had a great time," Gloria answers.

My stomach feels sick. I can't concentrate the rest of the morning. I pray that Mr. Blister doesn't call on me. At lunch, I run up and grab Gloria's hand. "What do you have for lunch today? I've got pudding. Wanna share it with me?" I ask.

"Sure," Gloria answers, "but Jooling will have to sit with us too."

When we get to the cafeteria, Gloria sits next to Jooling and I have to squeeze in between two boys on the other side of the table. "Hey, Jooling, what's the difference between an orange and a baby?" Gloria asks, and then answers, "Nothing is the matta baby." Gloria laughs so hard and long the whole cafeteria is staring at her. Jooling grins.

That's not funny, I think to myself. She didn't even say the joke right. Gloria is not funny. I'm funny. I'll show them both that I am funny.

"Gloria and Jooling, do you like seafood?" I take a mouthful of crackers and start to chew them until they are soggy and wet. Then I open up my mouth. "See food!" I start to laugh and choke at the same time. Sarge, the cafeteria lady, runs over. "Phoebe Flower, what are you doing?" Sarge asks.

"Oh nothing," I cough back to her. "Something just went down the wrong pipe."

"Behave yourself, Phoebe, or I'll have to write you up," Sarge tells me.

"That was gross!" Gloria says.

Jooling stares at me.

"Pass me the ketchup, please, Gloria. I need to use it for a minute," I say.

"What for?" Gloria asks. "You're through eating."

"Mr. Blister says you should practice using cursive handwriting every chance you get. I am just doing what I'm told, Gloria." I take the ketchup bottle, turn it upside down and neatly write my name on the table.

"Jooling," I say and point, "that says 'Phoebe'. That's me!"

"Phoebe Flower! Wipe up that mess right now. Then take this note to Mr. Blister. You will have no outside play. What's the matter with you?" Sarge blasts this so loud it echoes through the cafeteria. The two boys sitting next to me howl with laughter. Gloria and Jooling stand up and take each other's hands and walk out of the cafeteria together.

So maybe writing my name wasn't so funny, I think to myself as I sit in the time-out chair in my classroom. Mr. Blister is very angry, even though I explain that I was only trying to be a good friend to Jooling. I hate sitting in time- out. There's nothing to do but stare at the walls. I'm supposed to be thinking about what I did wrong, but if I didn't do any-thing wrong, how could I be thinking about it? There is some cool, shiny paper in front of me. I wonder if I could make a paper airplane out of it. If I toss it just a little, everyone would think that was funny, wouldn't they? I grab the paper and quietly make a beauty of an airplane. I toss it gently through the air. It sails down on Isaiah's desk.

"Wow, this is great!" Isaiah screams. "Who made this?"

"Phoebe," Mr. Blister says, "if you can't sit in time-out quietly for fifteen minutes, I am going to make you write one hundred times, 'I will never write with ketchup again'. Would you want to do that, Phoebe?"

"No, thank you, Mr. Blister. Then I would get a blister on my hand and then I would be Mrs. Blister," I answer, knowing for sure, that was funny.

For just about two seconds, before Mr. Blister throws his hands up in the air and screams, "THAT'S IT, PHOEBE!", I hear the class roar with laughter. I can still hear some giggles as I walk toward the office with a note in my hand for Dr. Nicely, the principal.

Just the Way You Are

I push open the door to the office and smile when I see Mrs. Walkerspeaking, even though I don't feel like smiling. Mrs. Walkerspeaking is the school secretary and we're good friends. She likes me.

"Hi, Phoebe, long time no see!" Mrs. Walkerspeaking waves to me as she gets up from behind her desk and comes over to give me a hug. "What have you been doing with yourself?"

"Hi, Mrs. Walkerspeaking," I answer back. "I have to see Dr. Nicely. I think she's really going to be mad at me today."

"Oh, don't worry, Phoebe, she will be very nicely to you," Mrs. Walkerspeaking says as she laughs out loud. "Did you get that joke, Phoebe? She'll be very nicely to you."

"I do get it, Mrs. Walkerspeaking! I get it because it's funny," I tell her. "As a matter of fact, that's why I'm here. You see, I told Mr. Blister that if I had to write one hundred times that I would never write my name in ketchup again, I would get a blister and then I would be Mrs. Blister and he didn't even smile."

Mrs. Walker grins, covers her mouth, and coughs.

"See, that was funny. You make a joke about Dr. Nicely's name and we laugh. I make a joke about blisters and Mr. Blister sends me here. He just doesn't have any sense of humor. That's what the problem is. Thank you, Mrs. Walkerspeaking. I knew you would understand."

"But, Phoebe, the ketchup, part . . ." Mrs. Walkerspeaking starts to say.

Dr. Nicely's door opens and I walk right in. I've been there so many times I know exactly what to do. "Hi, Dr. Nicely!" I say and hand her Mr. Blister's note.

What's the matter, Phoebe?" Dr. Nicely asks as she reads the note.

"Well, there is nothing the matter with me, Dr. Nicely." I start to explain. "Mrs. Walkerspeaking and I just figured out that the matter is Mr. Blister. He has no sense of humor. That is the matter. How can a teacher have no sense of humor? If I were his principal, I would tell him he has to get one before he can teach another day. I know Mrs. Walkerspeaking would agree with me, too."

"Phoebe, this note says you wrote your name in ketchup, threw a paper airplane across the classroom and then made fun of his name. Is that correct?" Dr. Nicely asks me.

"Well, it didn't actually happen like that. But, I guess, yes," I sigh.

"Phoebe, this is really getting out of hand," Dr. Nicely says in a not too nicely voice. "I am going to call your mother and see if both of your parents can come in for a conference. You've been having trouble in school for a while now and we need to find out why. Wait outside my office with Mrs. Walker and I will try to call your mother. If I can't get her on the phone, I'll need to send her a note."

110

I really didn't think it was a good time to tell Dr. Nicely that her name was Mrs. Walkerspeaking.

"My mother's going to be very mad," I say.

I step outside the office and my eyes start blinking fast. I don't want to cry. Mrs. Walkerspeaking gets up from behind her desk and comes over and hugs me again. "I'm so sorry, Phoebe. May I ask you, though, why did you write your name in ketchup?" "Well, Mrs. Walkerspeaking," I start to explain, "did you ever have a best friend who was pretty and smart and wore cool clothes, but—she was not funny? Well, I'm not pretty or smart and I don't wear cool clothes, but I am funny. Gloria, my best friend, wanted to be funny so that the new girl, Jooling, would like her. Gloria isn't funny at all, but Jooling laughed. I had to show Jooling what funny really was so she would stop liking Gloria and then Gloria would like me again," I say, feeling sad.

"Phoebe Flower, you are pretty and you are smart. When you grow up I bet you will be a movie star and I'll come to all your movies and say to my friends, 'I knew Phoebe Flower when she was in third grade.' " Mrs. Walkerspeaking hugs me again. "When you get back to your classroom, be the best Phoebe you can be. Stop trying to be like Gloria and stop trying to make people like you. Your real friends will like you just the way you are."

"Thanks, Mrs. Walkerspeaking, but I don't have any real friends," I tell her.

"Look closer, Phoebe," Mrs. Walkerspeaking smiles at me.

The door opens and Dr. Nicely comes out to tell me she has reached my mother on the phone and that I can go back to my classroom. I wave at Mrs. Walkerspeaking and she winks at me.

Math
My Way

"You're just in time, Phoebe," Mr. Blister shouts as I walk into the classroom. "We are about to play a game called math challenge!"

A game is fun. Math is not. "How can we have fun with something that is unfun," I think to myself.

"Okay, is everybody ready?" Mr. Blister shouts. "I need two team captains. They will choose the teams. I will pick a boy and a girl captain, but I want each of them to pick boys and girls. The winning team will get free ice cream for lunch on Friday, so please try hard. The boy captain will be Robbie Vaughn III and the girl captain will be Gloria Von Kloppenstein. Gloria, you may pick first."

I sit up straight, look right at Gloria and smile like a best friend should.

"Jooling!" Gloria calls. She doesn't even look at me.

"Phoebe!" Robbie yells and grins a big disgusting grin.

"What?" I say.

"Phoebe, Robbie just picked you first to be on his team. Go stand next to him and, please, no more trouble from you today," Mr. Blister sighs.

I have had bad days, but this has been the worst day I've had since I was born. Robbie and Gloria continue to pick their teams until every one in the class is standing.

Gloria only has two boys on her team and Robbie only has two girls. I don't want to be on Robbie's team. I know Gloria picked Jooling because she is smart, but that shouldn't matter. I have decided that Gloria is not very good at being a best friend.

"Okay, the first question is for Robbie since Gloria picked first. Robbie," Mr. Blister begins, "five pieces of coal, one carrot and one scarf are lying on the lawn. Nobody put them on the lawn, so what is the reason that they are there? You have thirty seconds to think of the answer."

"I know the answer," Robbie says after twenty seconds pass. "A snowman melted. I couldn't think of the answer right away because when Phoebe and I make snowmen we don't use coal. We use colored markers and push them in so they won't fall out. Then the snowman has colored eyes and colored buttons."

"Great job, Robbie. Now your turn, Gloria," Mr. Blister continues. "What is twice the half of two? You also have thirty seconds."

"Easy, Mr. Blister. The answer is two and one half," Gloria answers.

"Sorry, Gloria. The answer is two. These are tricky questions, aren't they?" Mr. Blister smiles.

Gloria stomps to her desk and sits down with a pout on her face.

"Okay, Phoebe, it's your turn. If two peacocks lay two eggs in two days how many eggs can one peacock lay in four days? You have thirty seconds."

"I don't need thirty seconds, Mr. Blister. The answer is zero. Peacocks don't lay eggs," I answer.

113

"Very good, Phoebe." Mr. Blister looks surprised. "Jooling, your turn. Listen carefully."

The math challenge continues until only two kids are left standing. One is Jooling and one is me. It's my turn.

"Phoebe, this is a tricky question. Are you ready?" Mr. Blister asks me.

"Fire away, Mr. Blister," I answer, wondering when I got so smart.

"A farmer had four haystacks in one field and two times as many in each of his other two fields. He put the haystacks from all three fields together. How many haystacks did he now have?" asks Mr. Blister

I think about the trip to the farm we took in first grade and answer, "Only one, Mr. Blister, one big one."

"Wow, Phoebe, you sure are good at these tricky questions," says Mr. Blister.

"Why do you think I picked her first?" Robbie yells from his seat. "I love ice cream!"

"Okay, if Jooling gets this right, then we'll have two more questions." Mr. Blister explains. "If, she gets it wrong, Robbie's team is the winning team. Ready, Jooling?"

Jooling nods her head.

"Jooling, how many two cent stamps are in a dozen?" Mr. Blister asks.

That's so easy, I think to myself. He gives her such baby questions. A dozen anything is a dozen. The answer is twelve.

"Six, Mr. Blister," Jooling answers.

I want to jump up and touch the ceiling and scream, but for the first time since I've been in third grade, I control myself, stand still and look sad for Jooling. I even say, "Ahh, that's too bad."

Robbie's team is shouting, "Yea, Phoebe!" I feel so smart.

"That was a tricky question, boys and girls," Mr. Blister says, "Let's not make Jooling feel bad."

"Congratulations, Phoebe," Gloria says to me on the way to the bus. "I'm sorry I didn't pick you first, but I knew you'd understand and I didn't think Jooling would. Are we still best friends?"

"Sure, Gloria. I understand," I tell her. I really don't.

I can't wait to get home and tell my mom about the math challenge. She won't believe how smart I am. When I burst through the door, my mom is standing in the living room with her arms folded in front of her.

"Mom, I had the greatest day! Wait until you hear!" I scream at her.

Quietly, almost too quietly, my mom says, "A great day? A great day? Is that what you had? So, having a great day means writing your name

115

in ketchup on the table, making fun of your teacher and being sent to the principal's office? PHOEBE FLOWER, that is not a great day to me..."

"But, Mom," I start to talk.

"... and Dr. Nicely wants your father and me to meet with her in her office next week to discuss what we should do about your behavior. Go to your room, Phoebe, and get your homework done right now. I am so angry I can't even see straight."

I run upstairs and jump into bed and pull the covers over my head.

Add, Subtract, or What?

For the next week, I try to be a perfect kid in Mr. Blister's third grade classroom. I get almost all my homework done. I raise my hand if I need to talk or sharpen my pencil. I only go to the bathroom twice in the morning and three times in the afternoon. Mr. Blister asks me if I'm feeling okay. I am thinking that if I do everything right, my dad and mom will have to cancel the meeting with Dr. Nicely.

Then, on Saturday, I hear my mom telling Amanda to clean her room because Dad is driving in on Sunday and he'll be sleeping in her room. I can't believe he's still coming! I've been so good at school all this week.

"Why's Dad coming?" Amanda asks.

"He and I have to go to a meeting at school," Mom answers.

I feel sick to my stomach. What do principals tell parents to do with kids that write with ketchup on the table? What if they send me to a jail and make me eat ketchup sandwiches every day for the rest of my life?

"So, Dad, when are you heading back?" I ask my dad as he tucks me into bed Sunday night.

"When we get this whole mess settled, Phoebe," Dad answers.

"Oh yeah, that," I answer, pretending the whole mess is about the broken swing set in the back yard.

Monday morning my mom and dad ask me to sit down on the living room couch because they want to talk to me. They tell me there is a meeting in Dr. Nicely's office at nine o'clock and "we" all have to be there. Mom told me that I will be riding to school with them. I start to ask who the "we" are, but then I have a picture in my mind of Mr. Blister running into Dr. Nicely's office and telling all of them that I have become the perfect student and they can all go home and forget about the ketchup. I like having that picture.

When Mom and Dad and I walk into the office, Mrs. Walkerspeaking stands up and shakes their hands. "I just love, Phoebe," she tells them. "If I could pick anyone in this school to come and be my daughter, I would pick your Phoebe."

"Thank you," my dad says, "apparently everyone at this school doesn't feel the same, Mrs. Walkerspeaking. Is that really your name?"

"No, but that's what Phoebe calls me, so it's fine with me," Mrs. Walkerspeaking says. "By the way, did Phoebe ever tell you about the time I lost my good diamond earring down the heater vent?"

"I'm not sure if she did." My dad looks at my mom.

"Well," Mrs. Walkerspeaking continues, not waiting for an answer, "I called down to Phoebe's room and asked Mr. Blister to please send Phoebe down to the office and help me figure out a way to get it out. Phoebe borrowed yarn from the art teacher and attached a safety pin and dropped the yarn and pin down the heater vent and fished the earring out in no time flat. I just knew she could do it! She is one clever little girl."

I smile at Mrs. Walkerspeaking.

"Thanks, but is Dr. Nicely ready to see us yet?" Dad says without

118

one tiny little smile.

"Yes, sir, Mr. Flower. You may enter her office now." Mrs. Walkerspeaking opens Dr. Nicely's office door.

Mr. Blister and Dr. Nicely are sitting at a round table with five chairs. I am so nervous I feel like I am going to wet my pants. I don't think Mr. Blister is going to tell everyone to forget the ketchup story.

"Please sit down," Dr. Nicely says with a big smile. "How are you today, Phoebe?"

"Fine," I answer. How does she think I am? I want to charge down the hall and out the front door and run until I'm in the next year.

"Phoebe, I want to talk to your parents about your behavior in school. I want you to know what we are discussing, so that it is not a secret. Mr. Blister and I are going to talk about the problems you are having. We want things to go better for you in school. Do you understand?"

I nod my head.

"You can go to your classroom now, but I want you to know what's going on here, okay?" Dr. Nicely tells me.

I nod my head again as I get up and open the door and walk as fast as I can out of the office.

I wait one whole day and nobody says one word about that meeting.

The night before Dad leaves to go back to New York, he knocks on my door.

"Enter at your own risk," I say.

"It's me, Phoebe. I just came to tell you I'm leaving for New York tomorrow. You know, Phoebe," my dad begins, "I just want to tell you one thing. You have to work hard if you ever want to make something out of your life."

119

"I know Dad, and I'm really trying," I tell him.

"Try harder, Phoebe." Dad hugs me. "I love you and I know you can do it."

After Dad leaves, Amanda decides to pay me a visit in my bedroom. This must be my lucky day.

"I know what's wrong with you!" she whispers, "I heard Mom and Dad talking in the kitchen just now. Dr. Nicely told Mom and Dad that she and Mr. Blister think you might have 'add'. They spelled it out 'A-D-D' because they thought you might be listening and they didn't think you would understand if they spelled it."

"You shouldn't have been listening, Amanda," I say, wishing I had been listening too.

"Okay, then I won't tell you what else they said. I won't tell you about how you have to go see Dr. Getset, and how you might have to take medicine and Mr. Blister is going to write notes to Mom about how you act every single day," Amanda smiles.

"Well, if I have 'add', then you must have 'subtract'. So just subtract yourself from my room, Amanda, right now. You are making me want to cry," I yell.

Maybe I do have "add", I thought. I did win the math challenge for Robbie's team.

Maybe "add" is a disease that kids who do great in math challenges have. Maybe it's a good thing to have. Maybe Amanda doesn't know everything . . . maybe she does.

Mom's Secret Confession

The next day, I get to the bus stop early so I can talk to Robbie.

"Robbie, wanna hear something awful?" I ask him.

"No," he says.

"Well, it isn't awful for you, but it is for me, so do ya wanna?" I ask again.

"I guess," Robbie says.

"Well, my parents had to go meet with Dr. Nicely on Monday to find out why I'm always getting in trouble and Amanda said she heard them talking and that I have an 'add' disease and I have to go to a doctor and take medicine and get notes home every day. Do you think it's because I won the math challenge?"

"Phoebe, why don't you ask your mother? She'll tell you," Robbie says.

"I guess I can, Robbie, but I'm sort of scared," I say.

That night at bedtime, I hug my mom so tight I think she almost stops breathing.

"I love you too, Phoebe. Are you okay?" she asks.

"I'm fine, Mom," I answer. "Do you think Gloria can come over this weekend?"

"I thought you and Gloria weren't getting along," Mom says.

"Well, we weren't, but I think it's because I can never have her over. She just forgets that we're best friends," I tell her.

"Did you get all your homework done?" Mom asks me.

"I added all my math if that's what you mean," I tell her.

"Well, not really, but that's good. Do you need any help with your homework?" Mom wants to know.

"No, I'm pretty good at add . . . ing," I say.

"Why are you acting so weird and saying 'adding' so slowly, like your tongue is getting stuck on your teeth? Did you bite it tonight at dinner?" Mom asks me.

"Because Amanda said I have the 'add' disease," I blurted out, "and that's why Dad came here and now I have to go see Dr. Getset and take medicine and get notes home every minute and I want to know what's wrong with me and why aren't you telling me."

"Phoebe, honey, let's have a nice talk," Mom says as she hops onto my bed and puts her arms around me. "I am so sorry I didn't say anything sooner. I know I should have, but your father said he would take care of everything and talk to you about trying harder. That's why I didn't say anything to you. We did talk to Dr. Nicely. We're concerned about why you are not getting your homework done, and why you have trouble sitting still and paying attention in class, and why your room and your desk are always a mess."

"But Amanda says I have 'add'. What's that?" I ask.

"Amanda shouldn't have been listening. It's A.D.D. and that's short for a Attention Deficit Disorder. That's what Dr. Nicely thinks you may have. It means that you have trouble paying attention, but it also means that you are very clever and you sometimes think in more creative ways than most people. Sometimes you start something and then you start something else without finishing the first thing and that creates your messes. You are very smart, but you don't know how to show it in the way that school wants you to. You know how you don't like to sit and do your homework and how you daydream and how you hate to wait your turn?"

"You mean some people *like* to do homework and be third in line?" My mouth drops open. I am shocked.

"Well, I guess they don't mind it like you do," Mom tells me.

"And I don't know what's wrong with daydreaming, Mom," I say. Yesterday, Mr. Blister told me to stop daydreaming, and I told him I had just remembered that it was Buddy Dog's birthday and I had to go get him an extra treat after school. I bet no one else in the family remembered it was Buddy Dog's birthday."

"Exactly!" Mom answers.

"So, do I have to take medicine and see Dr. Getset and get notes home everyday from Mr. Blister?" I wonder out loud.

"We don't know," Mom says. "All we want is for you to be happy and do well in school and know we love you. Dr. Getset just wants to talk to you and do some testing."

"Phoebe, I have a secret to tell you, too," my mom snuggles closer to me. "When I was a girl, I had problems in school too. I think I have mentioned this before. I would stare out the window and watch the clouds and make up stories in my head about the sky monsters.

124

I was quiet and didn't call out like you do, but I had a lot of trouble finishing my schoolwork. I do understand what you're going through, Phoebe."

"Did you have to go see a doctor and get notes home and take medicine?" I ask my mom.

"No, because, back then, there was no one to help me, Phoebe. My teachers just got upset with me and ignored me. I think they thought I was just lazy. I wanted to be a doctor when I grew up, but I didn't go to college because it was so hard for me to study. I had to read things over and over again because I would daydream and forget what I was reading. You are so lucky. People at your school want to help you." Mom hugged me tight.

"Do you think I'll ever do better in school, Mom?" I ask and yawn.

"Yes, Phoebe, I think that with everyone working together, tryi ng to understand how you think, and figuring out how you can get your work done, things *will* get better. Now get some sleep. Remember, I love you, Phoebe, and we are all trying to help you."

"Good night. I love you, too, Mom."

"Sleep tight," Mom tells me.

A Very
High Five!!!

About a week after my mom and I have our talk about ADD, Mr. Blister calls me over to the classroom door and says, "Phoebe, I want you to meet Dr. Getset."

Dr. Getset is bald with a white beard and mustache. I've seen him in school before, but I pretend I don't know who he is. "How do you do?" I ask. I heard someone say that once, on TV.

"I'm fine, Phoebe, and how do you do?" Dr. Getset asks me. I can tell he wants me to like him. I don't think I will.

"Come on down to my office, Phoebe. We can play some games." Dr. Getset turns and walks down the hall. Mr. Blister nods for me to follow him.

When we get to his office, Dr. Getset smiles and says, "Do you have any questions for me, Phoebe?"

"Yeah," I say, "is that really your name?"

"Sure is, Dr. Mark Getset, that's me!" he says. "I even have a dog named 'Go'. When I walk down the street with my dog, the neighbors yell, 'Hey, Mark Getset and Go.' Get it, Phoebe?" Dr. Getset laughs.

I guess that was pretty funny. Maybe I will like him. I wonder if I should tell him my Mr. Blister joke.

Dr. Getset is a pretty nice guy. He asks me questions and listens carefully to my answers. He asks, "Phoebe, what's your favorite thing to do?"

"Daydream, Dr. Getset," I answer.

He says, "I love to do that too, Phoebe, especially when I'm working in my garden."

We play games and he asks me questions and I have to do math problems in my head. He shows me pictures and I have to tell him what I see. When it's time for me to go I ask, "Dr. Getset, is there something wrong with me?"

"Not at all, Phoebe, you are a very smart little girl." Dr. Getset puts his hand on my shoulder. "You just do things a little differently, and some things, like paying attention and getting your work done, are harder for you. I have helped lots of other kids with these problems do better in school. What do you think about that?" "I don't know," I answer, "but it sounds good to me."

Once a week, I go to Dr. Getset's room. Today, when I see him I am feeling pretty sad and I don't know why.

"What's the matter, Phoebe?" Dr. Getset asks me.

"I don't know," I tell him. "I just hate coming to school."

"Phoebe, do you know why you are coming to see me?" Dr. Getset asks.

"Well, sort of," I answer. "Mom says I'm clever and smart, but I don't feel clever or smart. I am always getting into trouble with Mr. Blister."

"Let me try to explain, Phoebe," Dr. Getset says. "Do you remember how you rescued Jack and how you helped Mrs. Walker find her earring

127

and how you won the math challenge?"

"Yeah, of course I do," I tell him.

"Well, Phoebe, you were a heroine because you think in a different way than most kids, but that's why you get into trouble, too," Dr. Getset continues. "You like life to be exciting. It's hard for you to read textbooks and study spelling words and practice multiplication because your mind wanders to things that are more interesting to you. Then, when you have a choice of doing your school work or thinking of fun exciting things, you choose the fun things and that's how you get into trouble. Does that make sense to you, Phoebe?"

"Yes, I guess so," I tell him.

"Dr. Nicely and Mr. Blister want to help you. It's important that you do well in school and it's also important that you understand how you think," Dr. Getset says. "I am the lucky man who is here to help you. So, Phoebe, on your mark, get set . . . let's go."

When I get back to the classroom, Mr. Blister tells me that the class just went outside to the playground. I hurry out to tell Robbie that Dr. Getset is going to help me. Robbie is running straight at me. He looks like he is about to cry.

"Phoebe, you've gotta help me. Please!" Robbie yells. "Isaiah made a paper airplane out of my essay. He tossed it and it landed in that tree over there. Will you climb up and get it for me, please?"

I am trying so hard to stay out of trouble. If I get caught in that tree, I'll be in big trouble again. I know Robbie is afraid of heights, but it does serve him right. The essay isn't due for two more days. He always has his work done ahead of time. Robbie would do anything for me, though.

"Okay," I say slowly.

Hurry, Phoebe," Robbie calls as I head toward the tree, "the bell is going to ring in about ten minutes."

I pull myself up on the lowest branch of the tree. I can see Robbie's paper about six branches up. This is so easy. I don't know what Robbie's afraid of.

"Hey, Robbie," I hear a group of boys call, "come on and play football with us."

Robbie looks up at me and shrugs his shoulders and runs off to play with his friends. I reach the spot where his essay has landed and grab it off the branch. No wonder the paper airplane went up in the tree. Isaiah didn't make it right. I'll have to show him how to make it so it flies straight. I start to climb down the tree.

"Come on, let's sit under this tree, Elizabeth," I hear Gloria say. I look down and see Gloria, Elizabeth and three other girls from my class walking toward my tree. I stop moving and hold my breath. They put their sweaters on the grass and sit right underneath me. "Please, oh, please, don't look up," I think to myself.

"I don't know why you're such good friends with Jooling, Gloria," Elizabeth says.

"I think she can speak better English than she does. I bet she just likes the attention she gets."

The other three girls nodded their heads.

"What do you think, Gloria?" Elizabeth asks.

"She's okay," Gloria answers.

"Oh, sure she's okay, but she acts like she's so pretty and all the boys think so too," says Elizabeth. "I don't think she's very pretty at all, do you?"

"She's not bad," answers Gloria.

130

"Not bad, maybe, but I wouldn't be caught dead in the clothes she wears. Would you?" Elizabeth asks.

"I guess I wouldn't," Gloria laughs. "Her skirt is pretty ugly."

The bell rings and all five girls get up giggling and head toward the school.

"Wow," I think to myself, "I guess Gloria doesn't really like Jooling after all. She must have just wanted Mr. Blister to think she liked her. That is great news for me. Gloria and I can still be best friends." I hop out of the tree and skip all the way into school.

Tonight, I sit at my desk thinking it's the first time in my whole life that I'm excited to start my homework. I start to write the title of my essay, "I Am Most Thankful For My Best Friend." That doesn't sound good. I rip it up. "The Friend I Am Most Thankful For." "I Am Thankful For Gloria." No, it just doesn't seem right. I throw seven papers in the basket and stare at my desk.

I hear a knock on the door. "Come in," I say.

"Phoebe, can I help you?" Mom asks as she rubs my back.

"I need all the help I can get." "I just can't write it, Mom," I tell her. "It doesn't sound right."

"You might be thinking too hard. Writing about your best friend should be easy. Just write down what your heart says to you, Phoebe." Mom hugs me. "Call me if you need my help."

All of a sudden, I don't need help. I write my essay and then I sleep all night.

The next day at school, I wait until it's my turn to read my essay.

Finally, Mr. Blister asks, "Phoebe Flower, it's your turn to read. Did you do your homework?"

"Sure did, Mr. Blister," I tell him.

I walk to the front of the room and clear my throat. "I Am Most Thankful For My Best Friend," I begin.

Gloria turns, smiles and looks around the room. "We all know who that is," she whispers loudly.

"My best friend knows when I'm happy and when I'm sad. My best friend knows when I need to be alone and when I need a friend. My best friend helps me and I help my best friend, too, even when I don't want to. My best friend says nice things to me and thinks I'm smart. I don't have to pretend to be somebody else when I'm with my best friend. I can be me, and do things differently, and know that's okay." I look up and breathe. "Mrs. Walkerspeaking said, 'Look closer, Phoebe, and you'll find your real friends.' I didn't know Mrs. Walkerspeaking meant look next door."

Gloria's mouth drops open and her smile disappears.

"Robert Vaughn III is always first when I need a friend. I am most thankful for Robbie." I take a deep breath.

The classroom is as quiet as falling snowflakes. Not one kid speaks. Mr. Blister clears his throat, but doesn't say a word.

I shove my essay into my pocket and walk back to my seat. I have to walk by Robbie's desk. He stares at me and stands up. I stare back at him. I hope I didn't embarrass Robbie and he'll never like me again.

"Stop!" Robbie says. He puts his hand up. "High five, Phoebe!" Robbie smiles.

"High five, Robbie!" I smile back. That's what friends are for.

132

Part 4

That's What
Sisters Are For

Fabulous Phoebe

After I read my *Most Thankful For* essay and announced to the class that Robbie Vaughn III was my best friend, the strangest thing happened. I thought for sure that, for the rest of my life, I would be as lonely as my purple hoola hoop that's been lying on the garage floor for three years. I thought as soon as the whole class found out Robbie was best friends with a girl he would get on his bike and ride as fast and as far away from me as he could. I was also sure Gloria and Elizabeth would tell everyone what a loser I was to have a boy as a best friend. Then, of course, there was Jooling, but she never talked to me anyway, so there I'd be . . . me, myself, and I, all alone.

So when Robbie high-fived me, I was shocked. He liked the essay and said it was the nicest thing anyone ever said about him.

Elizabeth grabbed my arm on the way out the door and said, "Great essay, Phoebe, Gloria definitely did not deserve to be your best friend."

Jooling looked at me and smiled.

Gloria wasn't even mad. She said, "Phoebe, you are so funny. What a trick you played on me!"

The best news was I got a big A+ on the paper. Mr. Blister told me he was very pleased at how well I wrote. My mom and dad were so proud of me. "See, Phoebe," Mom said, "let your heart do your talking and you will always do well." That night Mom made me my favorite dinner of meatloaf and baked potatoes. When you have a great day like that, you want it to last forever.

"Why, may I ask, are we having Phoebe's favorite dinner tonight?" Amanda, my big sister, asked. "What fabulous thing did she do?"

"Yuck, meloaf," Walter, my little brother said.

"Amanda and Walter, we are having meatloaf tonight because Phoebe got an A+ on her paper today and we are celebrating," Mom announced.

"I get A+ on all my papers," Amanda said, "so I think we should have liver and onion sandwiches every night. That's my favorite."

"Yucky, yucky, yucky, poo," said Walter.

"In fact, Mother and Miss Brain of the Year," Amanda announced, "I am entering a contest and everyone knows I will win because everyone also knows I am the best writer in my class. I have to write a five page paper on 'What Makes a Good Citizen.' It will be judged on both how neat it is and how well it is written. When I win, I will be going to Washington, DC, with my teacher. Then you can eat all the meatloaf you want. I'll be eating lobster with the president."

"Please try to be happy for Phoebe, Amanda. Thank you for understanding," Mom said and smiled.

"So what was this fabulous paper about, Phoebe, brainiac?" Amanda asked.

"Well, it wasn't really that big of a deal. I just wrote about my best friend," I told her.

"What did you say that was so special about Gloria?" Amanda asked.

"Well, it wasn't about Gloria," I answered.

"I don't understand this conversation," Amanda said. "Who could it be about, Phoebe? You don't have any friends. Personally, I could never understand why Gloria spent her time hanging around you."

"Phoebe does have friends, Amanda," my mom said, "and her best friend is not Gloria, but Robbie. She wrote that in her essay, read it to the class, and got an A+."

"You have got to be kidding me!" Amanda stood up and screamed. "You didn't stand up in front of the class and say a boy was your best friend. I mean, Robbie's OK, but he's a boy. Are you crazy? How can we possibly be related?"

"Amanda Flower, one more word like that and you can go to your room. Do you understand?" Mom took her pointer finger and aimed it at Amanda's face.

"Yes, Mom," Amanda whispered.

When Mom turned her back, Amanda looked at me and mouthed, "You are such a loser, Phoebe."

I can't figure out why Amanda hates me so much. My mother told me that when I was little I sat on Amanda's lap for hours. She rocked and sang to me and read me books. Maybe she hates me for getting too big to sit on her lap. Some day I'll ask her, but certainly not tonight. Tonight, I'm afraid of what she might say.

Mom let Robbie come over and have ice cream sundaes with us. She said we could eat them in my tree house in the backyard.

"Hey, Phoebe, I've got an idea. Let's build some walls in this old treehouse and put some spy holes in the walls," Robbie suggested.

"We can get binoculars, and spy on everyone in the neighborhood and no one will see us. We'll be able to see right into Amanda's room from here, too."

"That's a very good idea, Robbie. It can be just ours and no one will know where we are," I answered.

"It will be so great, Phoebe," Robbie laughed. "I can't believe we didn't think of it before. My dad has some old wood in the garage and I know where he keeps his hammer and stuff."

"My dad is coming here for Amanda's birthday and a meeting with Dr. Getset next week so he can help us, too. I know he will," I told Robbie.

"We can hang out here, eat snacks, listen to music, play cards, and do homework in peace and quiet," Robbie said.

"Well, I don't know about that, Robbie. Doing homework any-where is not a fun idea for me. Plus, if I have to do some, I like to do it with loud blasting music," I told him. "It helps me concentrate."

"OK, OK, no homework," Robbie smiled.

I'll Be
the Teacher

Well, maybe no homework in the tree house, but I sure had a lot of it in the house-house. It seemed like I could never catch up. Mom was always checking on me, too. "Phoebe, did you do your homework? Phoebe, let me check your spelling. Phoebe, practice your math facts with me."

It seemed that Mr. Blister was only happy with me one or two days a week. I just couldn't seem to get all my homework done. Most days I couldn't even find the list of what I was supposed to do that night. I always wrote it down, but some days I'd forget to bring it home from school or it would fall under my seat on the bus or I'd use the list to wrap up my leftover lunch.

Everyone thought I was so cool for writing my A+ essay. That was good, except that I had a lot more friends. I began to learn that more friends meant more talking and more talking meant more trouble and more trouble meant more time in Dr. Nicely's office.

Last week in class, Elizabeth passed me a note about Gloria's socks. One was blue and the other was black. Gloria always, always looked perfect. Her dad even ironed her socks. Now that I think about it, it wasn't even that funny, but when I read the note, I laughed so hard through my nose that I snorted and everyone turned around to look at me, even Gloria. That made me laugh even harder.

I was still seeing Dr. Getset, the school psychologist, and we were becoming good friends. We would talk about school, my friends, my mom and sister and dad. I liked Dr. Getset because he made me feel that if he could pick anyone in the world to talk to, it would be me. What I didn't like about him was that when I told him Mr. Blister wasn't fair he said, "Now Phoebe, what would you do if you were the teacher?"

"Dr. Getset," I told him, "if I were the teacher, every kid in my class would have a swing instead of a desk. Before the kids in my classroom could go home they'd have to swing up and touch the ceiling with their toes. In my classroom, kids would have recess most of the day and work twenty minutes a day. If I were the teacher, Dr. Getset, when someone didn't do their homework, I'd take them to Disney World because that would mean that they needed to play more than the other kids."

He didn't like that answer, but he smiled anyway.

"Phoebe," Dr. Getset explained to me, "because you have ADD, it is harder for you to concentrate and stay focused. It's easier for you to play because it's OK to go from one thing to another thing when you play. If you're cleaning your room and you have to have it done before dinner, then going from one thing to another thing isn't OK because your room doesn't get cleaned and someone gets angry with you. The same thing happens with school work. Next week, when I meet with your dad and mom, we're going to talk about how you can stay focused on your school work so that Mr. Blister won't be angry with you."

"If you really believe Mr. Blister will stop getting mad at me, you probably also believe that someday it will rain orange soda, Dr. Getset."

"No, Phoebe, I believe it will be grape," he laughs. "Right now, Mr. Blister is trying some classroom changes. That's why he changed your seat to the front of the room and gave you a schedule to put on your desk. You know, the schedule you drew your tree house on?"

"Isn't that a great tree house, Dr. Getset?" I asked. "It doesn't really look like that exactly, but Robbie and I are going to work on it and when my dad comes to visit he is going to help us and we can spy on everyone and no one will know it."

"It does look like a beauty, Phoebe," Dr. Getset said.

I thought about what Dr. Getset said and I did notice Mr. Blister picked me to be the messenger more than any other kid. At first, I thought it was because he thought I was a good messenger, but now I think it's because he was trying to understand that I liked to move around a lot. I loved to get picked, so I'd go straight to the other classrooms and straight back.

Mr. Blister also put up a list of classroom rules on the blackboard behind his desk. He said, "Boys and girls, here is a list of our classroom rules. It will be easier for you to remember them if you can see them. I feel we all need to see rules to remember them."

Well, how did I know he meant only boys and girls needed to see them? I'm not sure what made me do this, but the day after Mr. Blister announced the importance of seeing the classroom rules, I saw a stack of those post-it stick-on notes on his desk. I grabbed a few off his desk and wrote one class rule on each one.

"*Phoebe Flower*, what are you doing?" Mr. Blister shouted in the middle of his lesson on sinking and floating.

141

It got very quiet in the classroom. I was sitting in the front row, so no one knew why Mr. Blister was shouting. "Turn around, young lady, and show the class how you spend your time while I'm teaching a very important lesson!"

I turned around and at exactly the same second every boy and girl in the classroom screamed with laughter.

"Mr. Blister," I cried out, "you said it was important for everyone to see rules to remember them. I wanted to make sure you saw them, too. The rules are behind your desk so how could you see them?"

"Phoebe, take those post-it stickers off your face this instant, go to the girls' room and wash your face and then go to Dr. Nicely's office and try to explain that to her."

Dr. Nicely didn't like seeing me again. She didn't like the reason I put the post-it stickers on my face either. She didn't even smile. She said I was being disrespectful to Mr. Blister and she was going to have to let my mother know. I begged her not to. I said I was being silly and I was so, so sorry and I would write a letter to Mr. Blister and beg him to forgive me and I would never do anything like that again. I promised, if she gave me one more chance, I would change forever. "Please, oh, please, Dr. Nicely," I begged, "my mom has been in such a good mood lately."

"Oh, Phoebe, you are lucky I like you," Dr. Nicely said, "One chance, that's it. I don't want to see you in here again, unless it's to show me something you've done well. Do you understand? I'll have to call your parents next time. I'll just have to."

"Thank you, thank you, thank you, Dr. Nicely. I'll never forget you for this. I'll even name my first child after you." I hugged her.

"Remember our deal, Phoebe," she sighed.

From that moment on, my life was going to change.

143

Father
Fix-It-Up

"Phoebe," my mom calls to me when I walk into the house, "Robbie has called the house three times in five minutes. Where have you been?"

"Oh, just outside playing hide and seek with Buddy Dog," I tell her. "What does he want?"

"I didn't ask him, but he sure seems excited about something," Mom says.

The phone rings again. "I'll get it!" I call out, "Hello. Yeah. Hi, what's up, Rob? Are you kidding me? No way! This is the greatest! I'm on my way!"

"What did he say, Phoebe?" Mom asks.

"He's got a computer," I tell her, "Do you believe it? Robbie's got a computer and he said I can come over and use it. See ya, Mom."

"Do you have homework, Phoebe?" my mom asks me.

"Just a teeny, weeny, little bit, Mom, and maybe I can do it on Robbie's computer. I promise I won't be long," I answer.

"If you go to Robbie's now, you'll have to stay in and do homework tonight, Phoebe," Mom yells after me.

Robbie's computer was more beautiful than my dad's silver and black Harley motorcycle he bought right before he and Mom got their divorce. We have computers at school, but I never used one without an adult looking over my shoulder. There were so many signs and words on the screen that I just stared and stared at it until Robbie started to shake me. "Phoebe, wake up," he says, "Don't you want to use it?"

"Sure, tell me how to start it," I say.

For two hours Robbie and I play on the computer. I write him a letter and he writes me one. We both write one to Mr. Blister. Mine says I am sorry for being disrespectful. Robbie asks him why an apple doesn't sink. You can erase anything you write by pushing a button and there's no eraser mark. We play Checkers and Concentration until his mother calls, "Robbie, time for dinner. Phoebe, do you want to eat dinner here?"

"Sure, I do, Mrs. Vaughn, but my mom's already started to make dinner for us. Thanks, though, and I'll be back. I love this computer."

"Anytime, Phoebe, anytime," Mrs. Vaughn answers.

At dinner, I tell Mom and Amanda and Walter about Robbie's computer. "It is so beautiful and you can do so many things on it.

If you don't spell a word right, it fixes it for you. You don't have to use a dictionary. Robbie says that someday he'll be able to write letters to people in different countries and get one back on the same day. Can we get one, Mom?"

"Phoebe, computers cost a lot of money. We won't be able to afford one for a long time. Besides, Amanda's birthday is next week and I've been saving all my extra money to get her something special. I hope you've thought about your sister's birthday."

"Of course, I think about it almost every day, Mom," I say and smile at Amanda, "I could never forget my favorite sister's birthday. I was just asking."

"I'm your only sister, Phoebe," Amanda says, "and, if I had my way, I'd only have a brother."

"Amanda, that isn't nice," Mom squints her eyes at Amanda.

"What do you want for your birthday, Amanda?" I ask her.

"Something you can never use if I get them, that's for sure," Amanda glares at me. "I want rollerblades. You can't even walk without tripping over something, Phoebe. You could never rollerblade, that's for sure."

"That's what you know!" I tell her, "I am the fastest runner in my third grade class, Amanda. I bet I can run faster than you," I yell.

"That's great that you can run, Phoebe. You just have to learn how to walk and you'll be fine," she laughs.

"Could we have one dinner without you two fighting? Please!" Mom looks down at her plate and takes a deep breath.

After dinner my mom says, "Phoebe," as she grabs me by the arm and pulls me into the hall closet, "I have saved up enough money to buy Amanda rollerblades for her birthday. It's a secret and you can't tell her. I want to hide them so it's a big surprise. Can I put them under your bed? She'll never look there."

"Wow, you really got her rollerblades, Mom?" I ask, "Can I see them?"

"Yes, they're out in the car and I'm going to sneak them up to your room. I spent a long time thinking about where I should hide them and I decided no human would even try to enter *your* room and if they did they'd have to be an acrobat or a gorilla to get to your bed and then, if they tried to look under your bed . . . well, that's a whole other story. Sometimes I wonder what's growing under there, Phoebe."

"Mom, I just cleaned my room last week," I tell her.

"Well, anyway, Phoebe," Mom says, "You can peek, but *don't*, and, I repeat, *don't* even think of putting them near your feet. You must have knee guards and elbow guards and a helmet before you wear them. Repeat after me, Phoebe, I will not think of putting them near my feet. "

"As Dr. Nicely says, 'You can't control your thoughts, but you can control your actions.' Don't worry, Mom, I don't want to touch those dumb things," I tell my mother. "I'm going to have a new tree house anyway. Dad is going to help me fix it up when he comes up next week. I'll be way too busy to think about silly rollerblades."

"Thank you, Phoebe. I'm going to jump in the shower, now. Will you watch Walter for me, please?" Mom asks, "I'll only be a minute."

"Sure, Mom, I love to watch Walter, but where's Amanda?" I am curious.

"She ran to the grocery store for me. We were out of milk. She should be back in a little while," Mom answers.

I want so badly to look at those rollerblades, but I promised my mom and a promise is a promise. I go play trucks with Walter, but no matter how hard I try, I can't stop thinking about them. That night I go to sleep and dream about rollerblading down the side of a mountain, doing flips and cartwheels as I rollerblade.

Dad comes on Friday night to celebrate Amanda's birthday. He is planning on being here for four days. I am so excited to see him, I greet him at the door with a huge bear hug. "Dad, you've got to come outside and look at the tree house. Robbie and I have great plans for it. I told him you'd help us."

"Easy, Phoebe, I just got here. First, I have to wish the birthday girl a happy birthday and then we'll go outside. I promise I will help you. How are you anyway? I heard about your A+ essay. Now, that's my girl!"

"I've been great, Dad! Robbie has a new computer and he lets me use it to do my homework and Mr. Blister said that was OK as long as I did the homework and not Robbie."

"Great news, Phoebe! Maybe someday I can afford to get you kids one of your own." Dad hugs me tightly.

The birthday party is really fun. Dad and Mom don't argue once. Dad doesn't get mad when Mom forgets where she hid the birthday cake. Even I think it's weird that she hid it in the dishwasher.

I don't care that Amanda gets all the attention. She loves her rollerblades even though she can't use them until Mom gets her a helmet and knee and wrist guards. I bought her some bubble bath, Walter got her an electric toothbrush and Buddydog got her some stick-on fake nails. Dad got her a pearl bracelet from some expensive store in New York City. He says she is grown up enough to wear grown-up jewelry. He also got her a guide book of Washington, DC.

"I hear my oldest daughter is going to visit the president!" Dad says with a giant grin.

"Yes, I am, Dad." Amanda brags, "Everyone knows I'll win. And . . . I also have an announcement to make."

We all stop eating our cake and wait for Amanda to speak.

"Since I am now fourteen years old, from this moment on, I want all of you to call me Mandy," Amanda announces. I will only answer to Mandy at home, at school, and with my friends."

"Mom, can Amanda do this?" I cry out.

"Can Mandy do this?" Amanda reminds me.

"I guess she can, Phoebe," Mom sighs and looks at my dad.

On Saturday, Dad keeps his promise and helps Robbie and me fix up our tree house. He builds a roof with shingles he finds in the garage and makes a rope ladder that we can use to climb up to the tree house. He tells us he has an old pair of binoculars we can use as long as we don't spy on the neighbors.

Broken Bones
and Dreams

When Monday morning comes around, I am nervous about the meeting Dad and Mom and I are going to have with Dr. Getset. I like being alone with Dr. Getset. My parents being there is a very different story.

"Hi, Mr. and Mrs. Flower," Dr. Getset says, "I am so glad you both could come in. Have a seat. I would also like to meet Amanda and Walter, too, and of course, Buddydog."

I can tell Mom and Dad are nervous, but they shake his hand and sit down.

"I know you are eager to get to the point of this meeting, so I will," Dr. Getset explains.

Dr. Getset is great! Both my parents laugh about his dog, Go, and how he got the name. Then Dr. Getset tells them that the results of my tests show that I have ADD.

"What we can do for Phoebe is our main concern," Dad says.

"Well, there are several things you can do," Dr. Getset says. "Mr. Blister is already using different ideas in the classroom to help her. Right, Phoebe?"

"Yes, he is!" I smile at Dr. Getset. I think he heard about the post-it stickers.

"She can also take medication. Several children at our school take it and it helps them pay attention. Also, I know of some high school students that tutor children from our school. They do it for extra credit, so it wouldn't cost you anything. That might help Phoebe take more of an interest in her homework."

"We can do that. Is there anything else?" Mom wonders.

"Well, Mrs. Flower, you can help Phoebe get organized," Dr. Getset says.

To my surprise, Mom answers, "I've always wanted to be more organized myself, Dr. Getset, and I know this sounds crazy, but I don't know how. If I have trouble, how can I help Phoebe?"

"Well, why don't you two work on that together? I have pamphlets that suggest lots of ideas to help kids and adults. If you are more organized, Mrs. Flower, that will help Phoebe." Dr. Getset smiles when he says that, but I feel like crying. I stare my mom's face.

Dad puts his hand on Mom's arm and tells Dr. Getset that Mom is a wonderful mother.

"Oh, I'm sure she is! You can't have a terrific, loving daughter like Phoebe, if you don't have a wonderful mother. Do either of you have any questions?" Dr. Getset asks.

"How will Phoebe take this medication if she's in school?" Mom asks.

"There now are several new medications for ADD that last all day. Phoebe can take one before she comes to school. You'll have to visit your pediatrician, though, before you start the medication," Dr. Getset explains.

151

"If you have any questions, call me day or night, here or at home. I want the very best for Phoebe, too!"

When I get home from school that day, Dad is packing to go back to NY, but he says he wants to talk to me before he leaves. He and Mom and I sit on the steps on the back porch. Dad knows this is my favorite place to sit.

"I like Dr. Getset, Phoebe, and I can tell he likes you, too," Dad smiles, "I know he wants to help you. I just want to go over what he said today so we are all on the same page."

What a Dad thing to say, I think, but I just chuckle.

"OK, first you are going to the pediatrician, right, Phoebe?"

"Righto, Dad, and there's no problemo there because I love, love, love my pediatricians," I tell him. I really do love both of them. They are the funniest doctors in the world and even when I'm getting a shot they make me laugh. Their names are Dr. Zach Black and Dr. Sue Blew.

"Before we go to the pediatrician," Mom says, "Phoebe, you and I are going to make charts to help us get organized. I have already been reading the pamphlet Dr. Getset gave me."

"And, Phoebe, your mother will be looking to find someone to help you with your homework," Dad explains. "Don't give her a hard time with this."

"Gotcha, Dad," I nod my head. No reason to upset Dad before he leaves to go back to New York.

"Mandy and Phoebe, I'm driving Dad to the train station and taking Walter with me. Can you two stay alone without fighting while I'm gone?" Mom asks us.

152

"Of course, Mother," Amanda answers, "I am fourteen and almost an adult."

"Phoebe?" Mom asks.

"Mother, you know me. I'm a terrific loving little girl," I tell her.

As soon as Mom and Dad leave, Amanda rushes into the house and up the stairs.

"Where are you going?" I yell after her.

"Where do you think?" Amanda yells back, "I'm going rollerblading, Phoebe, and you better not tell Mom. Do you understand?"

"Amanda, don't. If Mom finds out, she will be so mad," I tell her.

"Amanda? Amanda? Sorry, Phoebe, I don't know anyone by that name. Besides, I've wanted these for six months, Phoebe. I can't wait another day to use them. I don't care if I don't have knee and wrist guards and a helmet, yet. Those are for babies, anyway. You better keep your mouth shut, too." Amanda warns me as she sits on the front steps and puts on her rollerblades.

"I won't tell," I promise, "but don't say I didn't warn you." I don't mind being the one *not* getting in trouble for once.

I sit on the front step and watch Amanda wobble down the street. She isn't doing too badly for the first time on roller blades. She needs to stand up straighter, though. Amanda turns around and heads back to our house smiling and waving at me.

"Hey, Phoebe, look at m_____ ahhhhhhhhhhh!"

Amanda must have hit a crack in the sidewalk. She flies up in the air and lands hard on her side. "OOOH, AWH!" she screams. "PHOEBE!"

I race over to where Amanda's lying. "Are you OK? " I ask.

"NO! DO I LOOK OK? My arm, Phoebe, get somebody!" Amanda starts to cry.

"Mrs. Vaughn is a nurse. I'll get her." I run toward Robbie's, but Mrs. Vaughn is already heading towards me.

"I saw Amanda fall, Phoebe. Is she OK?" Mrs. Vaughn asks me.

I almost tell Mrs. Vaughn it's "Mandy" now, but instead I say, "I don't think so. She says her arm hurts."

Mrs. Vaughn helps Amanda sit up. She takes off her rollerblades and sets them on the lawn. "I'll have to drive you to the hospital, Amanda. Your wrist is swollen."

"Mom will kill me!" Amanda cries.

Well, no such luck, Mom doesn't kill Amanda. When Mom sees how much pain Amanda is in, she doesn't say one word about her using the rollerblades without permission. If I took those rollerblades, I would be dead and buried in the back yard by now!

The doctor at the hospital explains to Amanda that she has a fractured wrist and that she'll have to stay home from school for a week and a half and wear a cast on her arm for at least six weeks. Amanda sobs.

Two days after the accident, I discover I'm the one that should have been sobbing. I have to set the table and do the dishes by myself *and* I have to help Amanda get dressed in the morning. Now that's something to cry about! It's been nothing but "poor Mandy this" and "poor Mandy that."

"Watch my arm, Phoebe! Don't be such a klutz!" Amanda yells. "Mom, Phoebe is hurting me!"

"Phoebe, try to be gentle with poor Mandy. She is very upset. Her fractured wrist is the arm that she writes with. Now she doesn't think she will enter the contest to go to Washington. I know she's acting miserable, but you'd be upset too if you couldn't write," Mom tries to explain.

Upset! Is she kidding? What a great excuse not to have to do homework.

The next day, I overhear Mom on the phone. "Dr. Nicely, this is Mrs. Flower. My daughter, who used to be Amanda Flower and is now only answering to Mandy Flower, has had an accident. She won't be able to come to school for a week and a half. Dr. Getset mentioned having a high school girl tutor Phoebe, and I wondered if I could get the same girl to tutor Mandy and Phoebe. Do you have any twofers? Get it, Dr. Nicely, 'two for one' deals. Hee, hee."

How silly, a tutor, I thought. What can a tutor teach me that Mr. Blister can't? Just wait until she sees how smart Amanda is and how smart I'm not. I decide to keep my thoughts to myself. Mom has had one bad day after the other.

The next day after school, Mom takes me aside and whispers that she arranged to get a tutor for Mandy and me. "Her name is Constance, Phoebe, and she is in high school and she is a very smart girl. She will be coming on Monday, Wednesday, and Friday. She's in the living room helping Mandy and when she's through it will be your turn to work with her and I don't want you to give her any trouble."

Love vs. Hate

"Are you kidding me?" I yell. "You mean I have to go sit and do more school work? I honestly can't today, Mom. Robbie and I are planning to play solitaire on his computer. I promised him, and a promise is a promise. And, I'm not going to talk to any Constance from France with ants in her pants."

"That is not funny, Phoebe," Mom stares at me. "If you talk like that again, the next time you leave this house Robbie will have forgotten who you are. Constance is here for you because *you* have ants in your pants."

"Yes, and excuse us for listening, but Constance is here for me because I have the highest average in my class and I want to maintain that average," Amanda says as she enters the kitchen with Constance. "For example, solitaire comes from the word, solitary, which means alone. Robbie can play solitaire by himself. Constance, this is Phoebe. She needs a lot of help. She can't even remember her sister's name."

I really want to hate Constance, but she is beautiful and smart and she wears an ankle bracelet made from real gold. I know because I ask her. When she asks me where I want to go to do my homework I say, "My room."

"Where?" my mother asks and then looks like she might faint. But she smiles sweetly and only remarks about the "Messy Bessy" Phoebe that lives in that room.

"Cool!" says Constance when she sees the sneaker poster on my wall. "Where did you get a poster of twenty different kinds of sneakers? I like the blue high tops the best."

Constance helps me with my math problems. She teaches me to think about the problems and then asks me to draw the picture that I see in my mind. Then we do the number part. I love it when she reads the number stories to me. She reads like an actress. I can't wait for her to come again.

On Wednesday, I race off the school bus and into the house.

"Hey, Phoebe," Robbie yells from the bus, "can you come over today? I can come to your house if you want. Maybe we can play Chess in the tree house."

"Well . . . ah, I don't think so Rob, I have to check. I might have to fold some laundry for my mother. I'll call you!" I tell Robbie. Robbie is good at keeping secrets, but I want to be very careful that no one knows I am being tutored.

"So, Mom, when will Constance be finished with Amanda?" I ask when I walk in the door. "Doesn't Amanda have to go back to school soon? She probably doesn't want to miss one more second of work."

"Her name is Mandy, now. I know it's hard to change, Phoebe, but please try. The doctor said Mandy could go back after ten days," Mom explains, "She has to be very careful with her wrist, Phoebe. You do know she is *very* upset about not being able to write her essay and win the trip to Washington, don't you?"

"Yes, Mother, I am sad about that, too." I say, with my fingers crossed behind my back. I'm not sad at all. In fact, I am so, so, so happy that Amanda finally won't get something she wants. If she won that contest, I'd have to stick my face in ice water and freeze on a fake smile and pretend I think it's just absolutely wonderful that Amanda is visiting the president of the United States.

Finally, Constance comes into the kitchen. "Your turn, Phoebe Flower. What a great name you have! Do you know there's an eastern United States bird called a phoebe. It's brownish gray and light yellow." Constance smiles at me. "What kind of homework do you have today, Phoebe?"

"I have to write an essay on something I want to know about," I tell her.

"And what could that be?" Amanda asks.

"I want to know if all animals have belly buttons."

"Very, very cool!" Constance says, "Let's find out!"

Amanda rolls her eyes. "A bird name does fit you nicely, Phoebe."

When we get to my room, I ask Constance if she has a sister.

"Yes, I do," she says. "I have a sister and a brother, just like you, Phoebe. In fact, my sister and I remind me of you and Mandy."

"That's too bad," I tell her.

"Not really," Constance says, "I can tell you two feel about each other just as my sister and I felt about each other."

"So your older sister hated you. Is that what you're saying? And, you could never figure out why. When you were little she liked you, and read stories to you and let you sit on her lap, but when you got older she thought you were like dog biscuit gravy."

158

"Well, it was something like that, Phoebe, except that I was the older sister and for a long time I hated my younger sister."

"What happened?"

"Well, I finally figured out that I didn't hate her, I was just jealous of her and wished I could be like she was," Constance says.

"Well, there is no way on this planet that Amanda would wish she could be like me."

"I think you're wrong, Phoebe." Constance moves closer to me. "You are everything Mandy wishes she could be. You aren't worried about good grades. You are smart in ways she can't be and you are clever and happy all the time, even when you are in trouble. You are not afraid of anything, Phoebe. Mandy probably wants to be like you are."

"Constance, Amanda would never want to be like me. I get sent to the principal's office so much that I can tell you if Dr. Nicely flosses her teeth in the morning or at night, and that's not because we're friends," I tell Constance.

"I forgot to say funny, Phoebe. You are very funny," Constance laughs.

The next day Mom picks me up early from school, so I can go to the pediatrician. I laugh out loud when I see the sign in front of their office, even though I've seen it a zillion times. It says:

Doctors
Black and Blew
happily
take care of any boo boo.

"Hi, Phoebe, what brings you here today?" Dr. Blew asks me, as she grabs my chart and walks over to the table where I'm sitting.

My mom begins to explain what Dr. Getset told us about ADD.

"Well, Phoebe, I agree with Dr. Getset," Dr. Blew says. She takes her pointer finger and touches my forehead. "Remember that time you decided to ride your tricycle down the front porch stairs because you thought it would be faster than walking?"

"Well, sort of," I say, "I remember the blood, mostly."

"Yes, well that's what this scar is from," Dr. Blew continues to talk as she moves her finger to the scar on my knee, "Remember the time you jumped off the Merry-Go-Round before it stopped?"

"Well, I didn't think I'd get hurt from that," I shrug.

"That's why I had to put stitches right there," Dr. Blew hugs me.

"Yes, Phoebe, I have seen you in here many, many times since you were a baby. You are one of my favorite patients, of course, and I love to see you, but you are usually getting hurt because you're not thinking about getting hurt. Trying medication that Dr. Getset recommends is a good idea. Mrs. Flower, please call me in three or four days and let me know how Phoebe's doing. And Phoebe . . . please wait until the Merry-Go-Round stops."

The next time Constance comes, we skip backwards to the library together to find information for my paper. She says she has never done that before and she laughs all the way there. When we get back home, we go to my room. I open the door for her, do a spin around, and say, "Voila, Constance, do you notice anything different about my room?"

"Different?" she says, "Phoebe, it looks like an enormous brontosaurus visited your bedroom and sneezed all your stuff out the window. Where did it all go?"

"So you like it, huh?" I ask her feeling very proud of myself. "Well, I just got tired of the same joke."

"What's that?" Constance asks me.

"Mom would ask me to pick up my room and I'd say, 'I can't, it's too heavy'."

Constance laughs outloud. Then, she shows me how to draw some animals for my project. We work for about an hour without getting up even once. My mother asks if Constance wants to stay for dinner.

"Dinner! I just got home from school, Mom," I say.

"Time flies when you're drawing belly buttons," Mom laughs.

"Don't tell me that Constance is wasting her time showing Phoebe how to draw a belly button, Mom," I hear Amanda whisper to my mother.

The next morning, I can't wait to go to school and read my belly button story. I hop out of bed, jump down the stairs two at a time, eat my cereal in three bites, take my pill, and check my chart. I check off "make bed" and "flush toilet." Oh, rats, I didn't brush my teeth. I run back upstairs, brush my teeth and come down and check it off. I notice Mom has only two things checked off on her chart this morning. *Yeah, Phoebe!*

I'm on the corner before Robbie gets there.

"Wait a minute, Phoebe, what's up with you?"

"I'm up, Robbie, and ready to go to school and read my homework."

"Who are you and where's the Phoebe Flower who used to live in that blue house over there? The Phoebe Flower who thought her dog was a wizard, and everyday that Phoebe Flower would walk by her dog and say, 'Please, please, please, Buddy-wizard-dog, wag your tail, use your magic powers, turn me into a dog and I will be your loyal pooch friend for the rest of my life. Please Buddy-wizard-dog stop me from getting on that school bus'." Robbie falls to his knees and clasps his hands together.

"OK, Rob, you're right, I've changed. I realized Buddydog couldn't turn me into a dog, so I stopped asking him. But, he is the smartest dog I've ever known," I laugh.

"Phoebe, that's not what's changed. You've changed. You act like you want to go to school," Robbie yells at me.

162

"I thought that was the idea, Robbie. I thought everyone wanted me to want to go to school." I am feeling confused.

I think about what Robbie says all day. I can't believe I'm liking school. Do I really like school? I don't seem to mind it anymore. It feels good when Mr. Blister says, "Phoebe, I love seeing your homework on my desk." Then he marks it and I get most of it right. It feels good to feel smart.

On the bus ride home from school, I ask, "Robbie, do you want to play cards in the tree house after dinner?"

Robbie's so happy that I ask him, he pulls a pack of cards out of his back pocket and says, "Ready when you are, Phoebe! Come on over and do your homework on my computer after school, so your mom will let you go to the tree house after dinner."

Robbie must be missing me.

A New View

That night after dinner, we grab flashlights, binoculars, and a brown bag of peanut butter sandwiches and pretzels. Robbie fills up old water bottles with Kool-Aid. I grab a bag of M&M's that I had hidden under the couch. We climb up the rope ladder my dad made for us. It's as quiet as a falling snowflake when we get up there. We both close our eyes and count to three. Robbie guesses first. "I can hear the train. I think it's passing the mall. Can you hear it, Phoebe?"

"Yep, I do, and I hear Mrs. Burns washing her dishes. Can you hear her, Rob?"

"I think I can hear Prissy Fasola playing the piano. Do you?" Rob asks me.

"Yeah, but I also hear some weird whining sound. What do you think that is?" I ask him. "It sounds like a cat."

"Beats me, Phoebe. Maybe it is a cat. It could be a baby crying."

"No, I don't think it's a baby," I say. "Hand me the binoculars. Let me look."

"Oh wow, oh wow, oooh wow, Robbie! That's it!" I scream at him.

"What's it, Phoebe? Stop yelling. The world will know we're up here," Robbie warns me.

"This is why I'm liking school. I just figured it out," I whisper.

"OK, I give up. Why do you, now, like school, Phoebe?" Robbie asks me.

"Look out there into the back yard and tell me what you see," I say to him.

"I see lots of tree shadows and light from your house and a little sliver of the moon and a cat hopping over our fence and your car parked in your driveway and Walter's tricycle tipped over by the garbage can. That's about it. Why? What are you saying?" Robbie wonders.

"Exactly! I knew you'd say that. Now look through these binoculars and tell me what you see." I tell him.

"I can see into my house and my mom is eating dessert. She's supposed to be on a diet. Shame, shame on her! If I look closer I can tell exactly what she's eating. Munchy Crunchy chocolate ice cream, that's *my* favorite! But, what's your point, Phoebe?"

"My point is . . . looking through the binoculars is sort of like why I am starting to like school, Robbie. When you are wearing the binoculars you only see one thing, but one thing closely. Now, when I'm in school I don't see everything around me like I did. It's like my eyes have become binoculars and I see one thing and I want to learn about it. Everything about school seemed so hard before. Now it seems to make sense to me. I know why I'm learning stuff and I want to learn it. I read and I hardly ever daydream anymore." I grab the binoculars away from Robbie and put them to my eyes. "For example, now I see . . . now I see . . . "

"What? Come on Phoebe, what? What do you see?"

"Robbie, shh, look through these into Amanda's room," I tell him.

"Are you nuts, Phoebe? I'd rather spy on the president of the United

States than your sister. She'll kill us if she sees us. Besides you promised your dad you wouldn't spy on anyone."

"She isn't going to see us, Robbie. Just take a look." I hand Robbie
the binoculars. "Amanda's the cat, Rob."

"Wow, Phoebe, She's going crazy. She's throwing papers all around
her room. What's the matter with her?" Robbie asks me.

"The whole matter with Amanda began on the day she was born. I
don't think we have enough time to talk about that now, but I will tell you
what's the matter with her tonight. Amanda was planning to win the *What
Makes a Good Citizen* writing contest and go visit the president of the
United States and eat lobster. The contest is judged not only by what is
said in the essay, but how neat it is. Amanda fractured her wrist, so she
can't write and now she won't win. I'm glad because I won't have to hear
about how smart she is and Amanda is very sad. Boo, hoo!"

"Why doesn't she just type it?" Robbie asks.

166

"Because, Robbie," I begin to explain, "Amanda never learned how to type because her hand writing is so perfect it looks like it is typed. Every letter is just flawless. That's why all my teachers would say, "Oh, you can't be Amanda Flower's sister. She writes flawlessly. Why don't you try to write like Amanda, Phoebe? Then we'd be able to read what you write. Well, I did try and I couldn't and I guess it's too bad for Amanda, isn't it? That's why I am so glad you let me use your computer, Robbie."

"Are you just going to let her cry like that, Phoebe?" Robbie asks me.

"No, actually, Robbie, I was planning on calling the White House tomorrow morning and saying, 'Mr. Pres., my sister has a boo boo on her hand and can't come and eat lobster with you. I hope you won't be too disappointed'." I laugh so hard I almost fall out of the tree.

"Phoebe, I never knew you were so mean." Robbie shakes his head.

"*Mean! Mean!* How can you call me mean, Robert Vaughn III? I am nice. Amanda is mean. She has been mean to me all my life. She hates me. I don't hate her. I'm just so glad I don't have to hear her brag to me one more time about how perfect she is."

"Well, if that's true, Missy Nice Sister," Robbie stares at me, "then why don't you do something nice for her. First of all, try calling her by her new name."

For twenty minutes I sit and say nothing. Robbie says nothing either.

"What exactly is it that you think I can do to help *Amandy*, Robert?" I quietly ask.

Robbie shrugs his shoulders.

"Come on, Robbie, I know you are thinking something."

Robbie just sits and stares at Amanda sobbing on her bed.

"OK, you are going to have to help me, Robbie, and you and I could both get in a lot of trouble doing this, y'know." I remind him.

167

Robbie and I begin to make a plan. We decide that I'm going to pretend to go upstairs to bed. I wait for Walter, Mom and Amanda to go to bed; then I sneak into Amanda's room, find her essay, and signal Robbie by blinking my bedroom light three times to let him know I got it. Then, I tiptoe from my house to Robbie's house, where he will meet me at his back door. Then the two of us will take turns typing out a nice neat version of Amanda's essay, *What Makes A Good Citizen,* on Robbie's computer.

We climb down the ladder laughing and singing as loudly as we can.

"Phoebe, shhh!" my mother says as she opens the back door to our house. "Be quiet. You should be in the house getting ready for bed."

"As a matter of fact, I was just about to do that. Right, Rob?" I say and wink.

"Yes, me too, Mrs. Flower, I'm off to dream- land," Robbie says. "You should go to bed early tonight, too. You look very tired."

"Is that so, Robbie? Well, for your information I *am* tired, but I think I look pretty good tonight."

"Oh, you always look good, Mrs. Flower. Tired sometimes means good," Robbie says.

"That's enough, Rob," I whisper to him. "You're overdoing it."

"Well, good night, Mom," I say, and give her a big kiss.

"You're going to bed this early?" Mom asks. "Do you feel OK?"

"Yes, fine, Mom, I just got tired climbing up and down the ladder of our tree house," I explain, "Is Amandamandy around?"

"Tomorrow's the day her essay is due. I think she gave up trying to write it. She is so upset. I wish I could think of a way to help her. Maybe I'll go check on her."

"No, no, no, Mom, I'll check on her. I'll tell her some jokes to cheer her up."

168

"That's sweet, Phoebe, but Mandy has never liked your jokes. Maybe you shouldn't do that tonight," Mom warns me.

"Good idea, I'll just say good night to her. You relax, Mom. I'll take care of everything. By the way, is Walter asleep yet?"

"Sound asleep, Phoebe, so tiptoe upstairs, please, and thanks for being so kind to Amanda. I know she doesn't always appreciate you."

"That's the truest thing you've ever said." I hug my mom.

So far the plan is working better than any FBI agent could have planned. I open Amanda's door slowly and peek into her room. She has fallen asleep on top of her bed with her clothes on. Her essay is torn and thrown all over the floor. What a mess! How am I going to get all of it? I decide to pick it up now, while she is breathing heavily. I crawl into her room on my stomach and start to pick up the paper scraps one at a time. I finally have almost every single piece tucked into my tee shirt. Just as I start to crawl backwards out the door my foot hits Amanda's waste basket and knocks it over. Oh, no!

"PHOEBE!!!" Amanda screams, "What are you doing here? I told you never to come in here and I mean it. Now, get out!"

"Amanda, my bouncy ball accidentally rolled across the hall into your room," I lie to her, "I had to find it. I'll never come in again. I promise. Now, go back to sleep."

"My name is *Mandy* and you are such a baby, Phoebe. When are you going to stop playing with balls and grow up! Get out NOW!!" Amanda was yelling very loudly.

"Phoebe, what's going on?" my mom calls up the stairs.

"I didn't tell her a joke, Mom, I swear I didn't," I say. "I'm going to bed now, for sure."

"Good, and good night, Phoebe," Mom says, "I love you!"

Lost but Found

The first part of the plan isn't going quite as perfectly as we planned. I have to grab my right hand tightly with my left hand, so it doesn't take that torn up essay I have in my shirt and throw it in the basket. Amanda is so mean to me. How could Robbie have called me mean? I'm the nice sister. Why am I doing this for her, anyway?

Robbie is waiting, so I better keep going with the plan. All I need now is for my mother to go to sleep. I wait in my room for what seems like an hour. I sneak down the stairs like an old cat and peek over the railing. My mother is pretending to watch television in her favorite blue chair while she snores. Should I wake her up or just go for it?

I slither out the door without one single sound. I know, if I wanted to, I could make a great criminal. Robbie is waiting at his back door with his pointer finger at his lip. "Shh, Phoebe, everyone just went to bed. What took you so long? I thought you were going to flash your lights when you got the essay."

"Well, Robbie, after Amanda called me a baby and screamed at me never to enter her precious room again for the rest of my life, I took a trip to the bathroom and stared down at the toilet thinking how much easier it would be to flush this essay than to try to tape it together and type it for her," I tell him.

"Well, then, why didn't you?" Robbie asks me.

"I don't know. I guess I like being called, Missy Nice Sister," I laugh.

"Let's get to work, Missy," Robbie says.

It takes us a long time to tape the paper pieces together. We're missing about five small pieces. Good thing Robbie knows how to be a good citizen. He has soda and potato chips for us when we take a break. We take turns using the computer. It checks the spelling and says where to put the periods and question marks. When we finish, it's almost midnight, but neither one of us is tired.

"Phoebe, I've never seen you sit still so long or work so much without getting up to do something dumb like peel a banana or clean out the pencil sharpener," says Robbie.

"Enough about me, Rob. You are doing a great job, too." I am feeling pretty good about how I can help Amanda. " I told you, Rob, this kind of thing is easier now. I think Dr. Getset knew what he was talking about. I am smart. I just needed to concentrate."

"OK, now the final stage of the plan, Phoebe. Are you ready?" Robbie asks me.

"Ready as Cinderella was to find her prince," I say.

"Don't forget to signal me when you get to your room," Robbie warns me. "One flash if everything is fine. Two flashes if everything's not fine. Three flashes if you're caught sneaking in."

"I think two and three are the same, Robbie," I remind him.

"Well, don't forget, Phoebe, and good luck." Robbie shakes my hand.

I skip over to my back door and see that there's good news and better news. The first good news is that my mother has gone to bed. The better news is that she forgot to lock the door before she went to bed. She always forgets to lock it, but lately she's been trying very hard to remember to do what's on her chart. I hope she didn't check it off if she didn't do it.

I have a five page paper in my hand that has to get to Amanda's room tonight without one wrinkle in it. Soon, this paper will be in the hands of the president of the United States. I feel just like I did the day in gym I jumped rope two hundred and sixteen times and won the jump rope contest; except this time . . . I used my brain. I sit down on the back steps and take a deep breath.

When I get upstairs, I slide the essay under Amanda's door. I almost forget to signal Robbie that all is fine. I know he is probably waiting. I flash the lights once, then I fall into bed.

The next morning, I hear Mom calling my name to wake me up. I'm dreaming I'm in a jail cell, trying to escape with a peanut butter sandwich in my mouth. If I drop the sandwich I won't get anything else to eat for the rest of my life.

"Mandy, Phoebe, what's going on up there?" Mom yells.

I flop down the stairs and sit staring at my cereal bowl.

"Phoebe, eat!" my mom says.

"Where's Amanda?" I ask my mom.

"Very good question. She'd better hurry because her bus is coming. I think she is just moving slowly because she's sad, very sad," Mom says.

Amanda bursts into the room with, "Good morning, Mother, Phoebe and Walter!" She even pats Buddydog on the head. "I love you, Mom. You're the best mother in the whole wide world. Amanda kisses Mom on the cheek, hugs her and runs out the door with her essay in her hand singing, "Oh, What a Beautiful Morning!"

My mom sits down at the kitchen table. "OK, Phoebe, what's up?"

"I don't know what you mean," I answer my mother.

"Why is Mandy so happy today?"

"I didn't notice. Was she?" I reply.

"You know and I know and Walter knows and Buddydog knows that Amanda, Mandy, whoever she may be, is never, ever happy in the morning. Added to that is the fact that she is sure she's not going to win something. I was expecting to see orange and red flames jumping out of her mouth this morning, so don't try to fool me, Phoebe. I know you know something. I don't want to have to call Robbie and ask him. You tell me what you know."

I have no choice. I know Robbie would tell my mom the whole story, so I confess. My mom has tears in her eyes. Then she hugs me.

I hurry off to school, but all day I think about Amanda winning the essay contest.

After school, Robbie and I jump off the school bus and together we barge in the front door of my house. My mother is standing by the window holding Walter in her arms.

"Where's Amanda?" I ask.

"She's not home yet. I knew she was going to be late today because the judges were going to announce the winners after school," Mom explains to me. "I am very nervous. Let's all sit down and wait."

"Sit? I can't sit, Mom," I tell her.

All four of us start to pace. Even Walter walks around the living room in circles.

When we finally hear Amanda's footsteps walking up the front walk, the four of us jump on the couch and sit perfectly still waiting for the door to open. Amanda walks in and goes past us up the stairs and straight to her room. She closes the door.

We don't move. We wait.

Fifteen minutes pass and finally Amanda's bedroom door creaks open. She walks down the stairs and travels slowly over to the couch. She is biting the inside of her cheek.

"I'm sure you are all wondering what happened in school today." Amanda takes a deep breath. "Well, sad but true, I lost the essay contest." There was not a sound in the room. "But," she continues, "I also found out something, something very special. I found I'm not the only smart sister in this family. Phoebe, I think you're a little too big to sit on my lap, but do you want to come to my room and sit next to me on my bed? We can sing songs and read books together."

My mouth drops open. Without answering Amanda, I get up and move slowly toward her.

Amanda smiles at Mom and Walter and Robbie. "I bet you want to know how I figured out it was Phoebe who wrote my essay, don't you?"

They all nod.

"When the judges read, 'Amanda Flower, first runner up', I thought to myself, no one calls me Amanda, anymore, except my sister."

Amanda takes my hand and whispers in my ear, "Phoebe, can you teach me to skip backwards?" We smile and walk together into her room. That's what sisters are for.